FEVERED

DEVYN SINCLAIR

Copyright © 2019 Devyn Sinclair

All rights reserved.

No part of this book may be reproduced in any form or by any electronic or mechanical means, including information storage and retrieval systems, without written permission from the author, except for the use of brief quotations in a book review. No part of this book may be used to create, feed, or refine artificial intelligence models, for any purpose, without written permission from the author.

CHAPTER ONE

KARI

The sunlight pouring through windows hits the rose petals floating above the water. An invisible wind is carrying them slowly through an infinite spiral, and I feel the small pulse of magic connecting through my fingers, moving up my arms and down again deep into my gut.

It's a simple potion, a combination that a lot of customers ask for—beauty and prosperity. None of my creations will ever make anyone truly rich or beautiful, but they'll have just enough luck to make them feel special, and enough of a shine to make them feel gorgeous. At worst, it won't harm them, and the benefits depend on the magic I'm able to use that day.

Today feels like a good day, as far as that goes. All day I've been completing orders, and they feel *good* in a way that they haven't in a while. Maybe because I'm looking forward to something for once. I shouldn't complain; I've got a good life. It's just not the life I was prepared for, and I still miss my old one.

I pull my eyes back to the spiral of petals—I need to concentrate, or I'll have to start over again. The customer asking for this is waiting, and she's a new one. I don't want her to wait any longer than she has to.

Closing my eyes, I search internally for that little string of magic that's coursing through my gut and focus on it. I envision it becoming brighter, clearer, and more potent because today it feels different. Today I can almost feel where the magic is coming from, the source, from somewhere far away.

Light flashes behind my eyes, that thread of magic is suddenly a flame. It's like a flood of new power just entered my orbit, and it all comes rushing into me at once. I can barely control it.

It pulses and swirls and ripples and soothes. I've never felt magic like this before, and I can tell, somehow, that it's only for me. Bright, sunny magic that turns cool and spicy and finally a tail end of silver glitter. It's just a burst, like the most beautiful firework in my mind, and then it's fading, slipping out and into the spell and leaving me emptier than before.

My eyes fly open. The petals are swirling with terrifying speed, changing colors before stopping, freezing, and sinking into the bowl of water in front of me. I watch the liquid turn a deep shade of crimson, so rich that I could swear it's glowing before the magic slows and winks out as the spell finishes.

Holy shit. What *was* that? That's never happened before. I have no idea what this potion will do now. I've never experienced that level of connection, and as I funnel the potion into a bottle, I can feel the tingle of power in my fingers. I'm not unhappy, because that felt…special, but I'm not sure I can guarantee the effectiveness.

Suddenly I feel ill, sick and dizzy, and I have to hold on to the desk in front of me so I don't fall over. Like that magic is being yanked back out of me, leaving nothing but an echo. So, so strange.

I take a second to recover before returning to the front of the store, smile on my face. "All finished," I say to the woman sitting near the window. Potions and spells take a while to complete, so I've created a comfortable and homey waiting space for my clients. Overstuffed armchairs and bookshelves filled with magic recipes along with popular fiction. There's a circular fireplace in the center, the flames enchanted to keep the temperature perfect for whoever is near it. Plus, I have a selection of coffee and tea if the wait is going to be too long. We're a specialty store, so we're never so busy as to be crowded.

However, the woman currently sitting there is not like my typical clients. She's stunning in an otherworldly way and is wearing a dress that's more suited to the red carpet than my little shop. It wouldn't seem like she needs beauty or prosperity, but that's not my place to judge.

I'm pretty sure that she's fae. I mean, I'm not going to ask, but it explains a few things. I don't really care, the few fae customers I have are always lovely, and many of them buy potions to enhance traits that they already seem to have in abundance. I think the taste of magic reminds them of Allwyn—of home.

She rises gracefully from her chair and approaches the counter, and I can feel the magic rippling off her. She has to be fae; and a more powerful one than I usually encounter. Blonde hair curls down over her shoulders, framing her perfect face and dark eyes. She's staring at me in a way that most people would find uncomfortable, but it's not unusual for fae.

"So it didn't really go as planned," I say. "There was a burst of magic, something I don't usually have. It got caught in this potion. I'm afraid I can't guarantee the results of this. I'm happy to make you another one if that makes you uncomfortable."

Her eyes flick down to the bottle, and for a brief moment, I see a flare of interest in her eyes. "May I see it?" Her voice is rich like honey. Dark and deep, and I can imagine her being able to get whatever she wants with a few simple words.

I hand her the potion, and she accepts it with delicate fingers. She closes her eyes and tilts her head, almost like she's listening to what's inside the bottle. Motionless like a statue, enough time passes that I wonder if she's gone into some kind of trance.

Finally, her eyes snap open, directly onto mine. "This feels lovely. Thank you."

Okay. I clear my throat. "I hope you enjoy it."

She studies me for a moment, the ghost of a smile appearing on her face. "I'm sure I will." And then she's gone, disappearing out the door and into the afternoon sun soundlessly.

I wonder about the fae who come into my shop, why they chose to leave Allwyn and live here in the human world. It's not common, and from the stories, it's not exactly smiled upon. But still, I have a steady stream of otherworldly customers who come into the shop, and I want them to feel safe. So I don't ask. Even though I'm dying to. I've always wanted to see the land of stories—to explore what must be so much better than the human world.

The shop is empty, and I'm going to close early today because tonight is the gala. The official start of the season, and the biggest party of the year in the ballet world. Plus, both Emma and Odette are being promoted tonight.

I should be there with them, being promoted alongside them. I ignore the hitch in my chest at the thought, freeze it before it can overwhelm me. That part of my life is gone. At the very least I'll be able to see it happen for my friends. That's enough. It will have to be enough.

I'm cleaning up the ingredients I used for the mysterious potion and the remnants of supplies from earlier in the day when I hear the tinkle of the doorbell behind me. "I'm sorry," I say, "I forgot to lock the door, but we're closing early today."

"It won't take long," says a warm and familiar voice. I feel myself smiling before I even turn around.

"Well if it isn't Mr. Williams," I say. "Hello."

Kent Williams has been coming into my shop since the first day it opened a year and a half ago. We didn't get off on the best terms either. He's a cop

—a detective. He makes sure the small fae population in New York don't break human laws and investigates the crimes that have magical elements. Sometimes that involves tracking down magic users, and a magic shop opening up was the perfect stalking territory for him. Until I set him straight. My shop is no-man's-land, including the surrounding streets. I don't sell anything that brings harm, and I won't contribute to the tracking of anyone.

Once he agreed to my terms, we've gotten along perfectly. And thank god, because I think I'm a little in love with him. Kent is gorgeous and funny and smart and every time he comes in he manages to make me smile.

He leans his elbows on the counter, instantly drawing my eyes to the way his shirt stretches around his arms. I have to look somewhere else so I don't give myself away and start blushing and stuttering. There's a soft smile on his face. "How are you, Kari?"

"I'm okay. Almost done for the day. Going to a party tonight." I don't mention the burst of magic. As much as I like Kent, I don't want him to go looking for the source.

"Sounds fun," he says, and my breath catches as his hair falls into his eyes. He's got these delicious brown eyes that I can get lost in, and I swear to god it feels like eating a brownie sundae.

"I hope so. More likely to be painful and a little awkward, but there will be wine."

Kent laughs softly, "Sounds like I should take you to a better party."

That laugh makes me feel things deep in my gut. "As fun as that sounds, I have to go. It's kind of a business thing, or it used to be my business. It's a ballet gala. My friends are getting promoted, and I want to support them." He knows I used to dance, but he doesn't know the whole story. Not many people do. But I suspect he's figured out most of it from our conversations. I like that I don't have to spell it out for him.

"That's nice of you," he says. "Guess I'll have to take a rain check on taking you to a party then."

I grin, "You actually want to take me to a party?"

Kent catches my eye, and I feel myself go still, the breath leaving my chest. He's not teasing me now, face serious. "You know I want to."

Kent and I have been circling around each other since we met, parrying and flirting back and forth, neither one quite ready to make a move. I'm ready, though. I've been feeling it lately—the loneliness—

and his visits are one of the few things that make me forget. I could get used to having that around more often. But it feels so strange and so fast. Even though it's been more than a year. "Did you come in to buy something today or just in the neighborhood?"

"Both," he says, stretching up to his full height again, "I'll take any luck potions you have, and I wanted to say hi. It's been a while this time."

I blush and look away, "Yeah, it has." I don't want to let him know that I noticed.

"There's been a lot of work outside the city. Attacks on magic users like you. That's why I've been away. But I didn't want to be."

Searching the shelf for the golden bottles he wants gives me a second to catch my breath and wrap my head around this. It's the closest that we've come to admitting anything. I can't breathe. "Your job was so boring that you missed no-man's-land?" I put the bottles on the counter in front of him, still not meeting his eyes.

"You know that's not what I missed, Kari."

I swallow, rubbing my finger on a worn patch of wood, feeling the grain. Managing a breath, I sort the scents in my head, the mixture of incense and cardamom that I use in the common area. Pine and rose and thyme from today's work. And deeper, the undercurrent of wood—maybe cedar—and fog that is Kent. "What changed?"

"What do you mean?"

I rub my thumb harder into the worn spot, focusing on the pressure so I can get the words out. This shouldn't be so hard, not when it's something I really want. "We don't do this. You come in, and we flirt, and we don't talk about the line that we've never crossed. What changed?"

There's something in his voice that I can't name, "I'll tell you if you look at me."

It takes me longer than it should, which pisses me off. I'm not the shy girl. I can hold my own, but raising my eyes to meet his feels like moving a mountain. And then I'm looking at him and he's looking at me and I can breathe again.

"What changed?"

Half his mouth tips up into a smile. "Nothing. Everything."

"That's not an answer."

"It is," he says. "Nothing's changed. Because I've wanted this since you threw my ass out of your shop. And everything's changed because I see you're down today, and I was hoping that I could make you smile."

I fight against the impulse to look away. "How did you know?"

There's that smile again, and he leans forward, pressing his palms to the counter. "You don't think I know you well enough by now to tell when you're putting on a smile?"

Shit. I didn't think it was that obvious. I don't feel that bad. I really don't. That magic earlier felt amazing, and I get to see my friends tonight. But I can't deny that there's an ache in my chest and maybe I've gotten so used to this feeling. So much that I can't even recognize it in myself.

It's not a comfortable thought.

I manage a small smile. "I guess you do. Thank you." We hang in that moment for what feels like forever, until I realize that I can't. Not tonight. "I wish I could let you take me to a party, Kent."

He smirks, grabbing the pen that's sitting on the counter and one of the many sticky notes I keep around for jotting down orders. "We've waited this long," he says, scribbling, "I think we can hang on a few more days."

"I suppose so," though I'll admit that I'm tempted to ditch everyone at the gala for this. If it were anyone but Emma and Odette, I would say fuck the gala.

He slides the note across to me, and I see that it's his number. "That's in case you need cheering up. Or anything else, really."

A laugh bursts out of me. "It's amazing that we haven't done this yet."

"Not as amazing as it's going to be now that we've done it," Kent says with a wink.

I shake my head, "Smooth, Mr. Williams."

"I try." He steps towards the door and I follow him, watching as he exits. He turns back as I go to lock it, and I peek out for just a second, feeling the late evening breeze hit my skin. "Really, Kari, if you need anything."

"I'll call you even if I don't."

The smile on him blazes brighter than the setting sun as he walks backwards down the sidewalk, almost crashing into someone. He's laughing as he turns away and I'm laughing as I lock the door to the shop.

I'm both looking forward to this gala and dreading it in equal measure, but either way, it's still time to get ready.

CHAPTER TWO

KARI

As soon as the door is closed, I put Kent's number into my phone and send him a text so he has my number too.

There's a text waiting from Odette as well:

> I can't wait to see you! Let me know when you're on your way.

I'm excited to see her too. It's been a little while, and she's going to be busy this season. There's a big part of me that's trying not to think about that. Or trying to figure out ways to keep myself busy so that I won't notice as much.

Making sure the sign on the front door is flipped to closed, I grab my bags from behind the counter and retreat to the bathroom. I brought all the stuff with me to get ready here, because going all the way back to Queens and coming back to Lincoln Center is not a trip that I'm willing to make. Not when I'm only ten blocks away.

The dress I'm going to wear tonight is one that's been in my closet for a while. It's actually the dress I had planned on wearing to my own promotion gala before it became clear that that would never happen. If Odette knew that she'd probably kill me, but I don't exactly have a lot of events to dress up for anymore, and it deserves to be worn.

I don't think I've worn a dress since the surgery. I've had no reason to, and I don't want to see the scars that took everything. Swallowing, I pull that train of thought in. It wasn't the surgery that made it so I can't dance. It was my own stubbornness and moving far too fast. But sometimes it's easier to tell myself that it was the surgery. I shake my head. I can't think about this or I won't come out of the spiral.

I pull it out of the garment bag and hang it on the back of the door, giving it the chance to work out any last wrinkles. I love this dress. It's a dove grey silk gown that slips off my shoulders and exposes my back before smoothly draping all the way down to my feet. It's simple and gorgeous and gives that rare feeling of walking on air when you wear it. So I'm not going to let it sit in my closet.

Besides, wearing it tonight might give me some closure.

At least I hope that it will.

I do my hair and make-up first, and there's a calm that comes over me as I do it—an air of ritual that comes from years of doing my hair and make-up before performances. I miss that. My new everyday life rarely calls for me to look fancy, and when you're making potions and charms, it's usually better to have your hair out of the way. I curl my hair and leave it spiraling over my shoulders. By the time I get to the gala, it will have relaxed into my favorite kind of wave.

My eyes take a while—the smoky eye you learn to perfect early on as a dancer. This is a chance for me to be dramatic, and the colors I use are black and purple to make my eyes look more green and a touch of silver to play off the dress. I've always been good at this, and I love the way this looks. It's a pity that Kent left already because I'd like him to see me look like this. Granted, I'd probably be a blushing idiot again, but it's a chance I'm willing to take.

The dress and the shoes are last, along with a light wrap. I poke around the shop for a few minutes. Partially because I am always ready too early, and partly because I'm still searching for a way to delay the inevitable. But there's not a much that I can do in this dress—certainly no magic work—and I have to admit to myself that I'm just procrastinating. So I grab my little purse, take a deep breath, and lock the shop behind me.

The sun is starting to set, and the late summer weather is perfect. It's warm enough to be beautiful, with just enough of the early fall chill that I'll be glad to have the wrap later. One of my favorite things about New York is the fall, and I can just smell the beginnings of it on the breeze. It's comforting.

I text Odette that I'm on the way, and head towards Lincoln Center, but I take the back way. Not down Broadway. There are fewer cars the way I go, and I get to sneak into Lincoln Center through Hearst Plaza with the trees and fountains and statues. It's one of the places I love most in the city, and I still spend a lot of time there. I ate lunch there last week.

I know that I'm thinking about the little things to distract myself from what I'm walking into. This isn't going to be easy. Plenty, if not most of the people there will be happy to see me. But it won't be that. It'll be the pitying looks and the whispers that are bound to follow me around the room. After all, I'm still the latest tragedy of American Ballet

Theatre. Even if my friends don't talk behind my back, the donors will.

Not to mention that I'll see my former sponsors and have to know that they're sponsoring someone else. This is going to be painful either way.

Once again, the thought enters my mind: I could call Kent and bail. There's no doubt in my mind that he could take me to a party that would wipe away every sad feeling that I'm holding onto, and that's incredibly appealing right now. But I would feel awful if I weren't there to support my friends. Besides, I've just turned the corner and can see the back side of Hearst Plaza.

I'm almost there.

My phone buzzes, and it's a message full of hearts and smileys from Odette, and it lifts my spirits for a second. I'm turning the corner behind the fake grass hill when I hear a voice behind me. "Excuse me!"

I turn, and a woman in a long black dress is coming down the block. She looks fancy enough that it's possible she might also be heading to Lincoln Center. She waves a hand, and I stop. Does she need directions? It takes me a second, but as she approaches, I recognize my customer from earlier—the mysterious blonde I sold the overpowered potion to. She's practically glimmering, and I wonder if she's already taken it and there were bad side effects. Guilt and nerves twist in my gut. I hope nothing awful happened.

She comes closer, and when I think she can hear me clearly, I call out to her. "Hi," I say. "Was there something wrong with the—"

She thrusts her hand out, and the magic hits me hard, a spear of crimson light straight to my torso. Pain erupts through my skin. Fire and fractures and screaming. There's no air left in the world—I can't breathe. Until the light disintegrates and I feel the magic crackle through me and to the ground like I'm a lightning rod. My lungs heave in a breath and I see that crimson light swimming across her hands. It's the same color as the potion I sold her, and as I feel the ability to move come back, I know that I've very much misunderstood what's happening here.

I need to get to people. Somehow, in the middle of New York, we're alone on the street, and I need someone to see me. Just need to get around the corner. She's staring at me with the same dead gaze, but now, in the reflection of magic, it's sinister. She's faster than I am, but I can't just let this happen—I have to try.

And so I run. My limbs feel like they're swimming in cement, and I'm unsteady on my feet. Magic connects directly with the skin of my back and pain ripples, triggers, makes me freeze and gasp. I should be screaming. Why can't I scream? I can't think.

My phone, I have my phone. It's in my hand. The texts are open and Kent's number is right there. He said I could call him for *anything* and this is *everything*.

Agony is all there is. I have to look down at my arms to make sure that they're not splintering open. Shit, I think my bones are breaking. That's how it feels, like being pulled apart a piece at a time.

I force myself to haul in air, to think through the pain, to stop myself from panicking as I see the tendrils of red magic curling over my skin, sinking in, burning. I'm being crushed and mutilated, even if I can still see that I'm whole.

The wall next to me comes closer. No, it's not moving, *I'm* moving, falling. The grit of the stone under my palm brings me a moment of focus and I hit dial. I can't get the phone to my ear, but I can hear it ringing. Please please please pick up. My hand slips, and I fall. The stones under my hand are wet. Did it start to rain? Is there blood? It's my blood isn't it.

There's a soft, steady click of shoes on stone. She's following me. Slowly. Unconcerned with me running or getting away. The only other sound is my heart is pounding in my ears, like the ocean is roaring around me.

"Hello?" A voice seeps through the ocean of sound and pain.

Kent. It's Kent. "Help," I say, but it feels like I'm choking. "I need help. Please—" and then I can't speak, thick crimson smoke invading my mouth and clogging my throat. It tastes like bitter orange and ash and something rotten.

I can't breathe. *I can't breathe.*

I'm on the ground, and I'm dying. I know this. The magic that's slithering around me is pulling everything that I am away from myself. It burns. I've never felt anything like this before, like being tied to hot coals without heat, pain without impact.

She's above me, I can see her now, hand extended, red tendrils flowing from her palm to where they crawl over me with a will of their own before being pulled back into her. And along those lines, I can see light. Lavender and sapphire and pure gold. I know in my heart that it's me. She's taking my essence, my magic, and my life and there's going to be nothing left.

I can't feel anything. Can't react. Only stare at her face, which shows nothing. No remorse or acknowledgment that she's killing me. She wears a mask of indifference, and it's going to be the last thing I see. I wish it were anything else.

My lungs are bursting, but I can't inhale. The world is blurry and fading. I can only hear as everything fades to white. There's a scuff from her shoe on the pavement and the low, slick, sound of absorption.

Below the pain, is terror. This can't be the end. It's too easy. I should have fought harder. Should have done something—anything—to fight back. This isn't the way that I thought that I would die. Please. I don't want to die.

Stone cracks and flesh snaps. There are sounds of pain and a struggle, and maybe words. Every sense is searing with pain, but I blink, and I can see. The sky is a faded blue like the world has dimmed, but I'm not blind anymore.

A tiny gasp of breath makes it into my lungs. The pain relents a fraction. But I'm still dying—of that, I have no doubt. I close my eyes and let go. I let the pain fade into nothing as I fall into the dark.

I didn't think that death would be so peaceful, that feeling the life being drained from my body would feel like easing from one state to another. I always thought it would be a sharp distinction.

Light and energy pour into my chest, and I gasp

for air, my eyes flying open. The world looks normal. There's color and sound, and my entire body is still on fire. I'm burning alive again, and there's nothing I can do. I can't even find my voice to scream.

She's gone, but I'm not alone. Three men—three fae—are hovering over me. One is touching me, and I can feel pure white brightness emanating from his hand, cooling the fire, soothing the pain.

Who are you?

I try to speak, but my voice is nowhere. Pure pain spikes through the middle of my chest again and I crack open. Now I scream for real, and my world plunges into black.

CHAPTER THREE

BRAE

What the hell *was* that?

The remnants of dark magic crawl across my skin like a sickness. The fae who was the source of the darkness is long gone, and I would be tracking her down now if not for the human woman in front of me.

This is the last thing I expected. We rarely venture away from Allwyn, and a rare outing for pleasure turning into a nightmare was not the plan. But I couldn't hesitate when I felt that magic. It was pungent and vile, raising the nausea I now feel in my stomach.

That kind of magic shouldn't exist at all, let alone in the human world.

When we crossed the barrier into the human

world, I felt a swell of magic, but this was not the source. That was different. Peaceful and calming. The magic I'm trying to control right now is anything but that.

I've never seen that fae before, but I won't forget her face. Not now. She was stripping the magic and life from this woman—a stunningly beautiful woman—and we were nearly too late.

But she's alive, and I can't breathe because I can *feel* her.

Beneath the curse that's killing her, there is something more. The magic under her skin resonates through me like a bell, and I know that the woman lying broken in front of me is about to alter my universe.

Glancing towards Verys and Aeric, I see the same look of astonishment on their faces. This woman is special, and we can all feel it. She's calling to me in a way I already know, but don't want to put words to. Because it's impossible. Especially if we're all feeling it. Can it be?

Who the hell is this woman?

I sweep our surroundings with my senses and get nothing. There's no trace of the fae or her magic. I want to find her, but I can't because this woman is still dying—I can feel that too—but I'm no healer.

There's a pull deep in my gut. A terror that I'm choosing to ignore. She can't die. I will not let her die. I can't.

Nodding to Verys to keep watch, I reach out with my magic, trying to figure out what exactly has been done to her. The feeling is like a black hole in the center of my mind. It seethes and breathes and never lets up in its hunger. Everything that is in her is being drowned out and pulled away.

But there's something else. Almost like an echo or an afterthought, away and to the side. It's a tether.

"It's connected to the human realm," I say. It's soft, but they hear me.

"What do you mean?" Verys asks.

I lock eyes with him. "I mean I think that we have a chance to save her, but it's not here. She has to be in Allwyn. We have to get her to Urien. Now."

Verys shifts his eyes back to her still figure, and nods. Aeric isn't looking. His eyes are on the empty street around us. "We need to go."

He's right. We've been lucky so far, but that may not last.

There's a harsh click behind me, and Aeric turns too late. "You're not going anywhere."

There's a gun pointed at Aeric's head, and I

stand, seeing the human man that's holding it. I can sense his emotions from here, even though he's keeping them visibly in check. He knows this woman—is terrified for her—and he hates faeries.

Even if I couldn't sense his emotions, the sneer on his face makes that clear.

He's drawn the wrong conclusion, and I can understand why. Walking up to three fae males over an unconscious woman isn't an image that inspires a lot of confidence. "She was attacked," I say, "but not by us. We felt the attack and came to stop it."

"I'm sure that's true," the man says, tone dripping with disdain. "I've heard that before. You are all the same. It was an accident. I didn't mean to overpower the poor human."

The gun he's holding isn't an ordinary gun. I've seen one before. It's soundless and doesn't fire metal bullets. No, those bullets are made out of ash wood, and he's about to fire.

The sound the gun makes is soft, but Aeric is already moving, ducking under the shot and pinning the man to the ground. The sound of his flesh hitting the ground isn't pleasant, but it's necessary. I reach out and bind him with my power. I can feel him recoil from the sensation, and I realize I'm breaking a cardinal rule of our travel here: never to use magic on humans. But we have no time.

"Listen to me," I say as Aeric removes the gun from the man's hand and tosses it into the nearby bushes. Anyone slower than Aeric would have been dead from that bullet. "I can feel that she's important to you," I say to the man who's fighting my hold with everything that he's got. "I'm not a healer, and she is dying. The curse she was attacked with is draining her, and if we don't take her to Allwyn now, she'll be dead in less than an hour. If you don't believe us, that's too bad."

I lean down and gently place my hand on her chest. The breaths that I feel under my palm are shallow. Barely there.

The expression of her face is peaceful, but I've seen this kind of peace before, and it's death and not sleep. Still, she is beautiful, her fiery red hair spread across the pavement like a bloody halo.

Closing my eyes, I pour magic into her, directly into that void. It's raw and unshaped, but it's the best I can do while she's unconscious. The curse will feed on that for a little while, until we can make other arrangements.

Standing again, I look at the man, still straining against the magic. The look on his face screams murder if I touch her again. My magic is weakening, waning with what I gave to her and keeping him still when he's fighting to break free and kill me. "What's your name?"

"Kent Williams," he grits out. "And you're not taking her anywhere without me."

"What's her name?" I ask calmly.

"Kari Taylor."

I lean down so I can look him in the eye. "Do you want her to die?"

I can see the impulse to hurt all of us in his eyes, but it fades with his answer. "No."

"And you understand that if we don't take her now, she will?"

"Yes."

Aeric puts a hand on my shoulder, voice incredulous. "You're going to let him come too?"

"Do you want this fight right now? I can't let her die." I shove down the terror again, and what it means. No matter how impossible.

"Neither can I," he says, like the words are pulled from him unbidden.

"I'm going to let you up," I tell Kent. "And then we have to go."

Releasing the magic all at once, he shudders with the energy that he put into fighting stillness. But then he's on his feet. Every inch of his body speaks to the fact that he wants to kill us, but his eyes are on the woman. Kari.

I nod to Verys.

Slowly, he picks her up. He's gentle with her, and when he looks at me, I see my own terror written in his eyes. "You ready?"

He nods.

I look at Kent. "We're going to have to run."

CHAPTER FOUR

KARI

I loved to float when I was a kid. In the pool, when everyone else was always jumping and diving and swimming, I would float. On my back, ears under the water. I liked the peace of having everything blocked out and letting the flow of the water move you. The motion I feel right now is like floating.

But this has to be a dream, because I'm being carried by an angel. Pale skin, shining, silver hair, and a face that could be on any cathedral mural. I died. That fae female attacked me, and I died, and now an angel who's gorgeous enough to make me swoon is carrying me to heaven.

Pain rises up from the fog and seeps along my limbs, filling them up until everything aches. It's an ache that feels deep, like I'm rotting from the inside out. I didn't think that death would be this painful. I try to move one of my hands, and I find that it weighs too much for me to lift. Not only that, but the effort sends splintering fire up my arm and into my shoulder. It's agony, and I gasp. I would scream, but my voice seems to be elsewhere.

The angel looks at me and notices that I'm awake. "Brae," he says, in a voice that's deep and rich. That's not a word that I know, but I can't even ask because I can't speak. He lays me on the ground, leaning against a tree and there's commotion from behind another one. The angel is crouching in front of me, looking at me. Even his eyes are silver, and they're beautiful. I'd be smiling at him if everything wasn't on fire.

"Kari!" Kent barrels around the tree and is suddenly close. "Are you all right?"

I'm so confused. My brain is muddled, trying to connect the dots. Kent is here too? I close my eyes and fight against the way my body feels like it's shredding itself apart. "Am I dead?" The words feel strange on my tongue, like they're not coming from me.

"No, you're not dead," Kent says, "but you were attacked."

His hands are on my arms and no no no it hurts, and everything fades to grey. She's back. The pain is back. He has to be lying. I'm dead—or I will be soon.

"Back up," I hear another voice say, and Kent curses under his breath but his hands leave my skin. "She can't take the touch right now," the voice says. I try to open my eyes and there's another angel. This one's golden. Tan skin and golden brown hair and green eyes that are looking into mine. "Try to drink," he says, holding a bottle to my lips.

Drinking feels good, the sweet coolness of water a welcome distraction from the pain. I want more, but he pulls it back. "You have to go slowly."

A third man is standing back, and I think I'm going mad. He's got green skin, and hair so dark it looks black, but where the sun hits it, I can see the emerald reflection. It clicks in my head, then. They're not angels. They're fae. The fae males I saw over me. I glance towards this male's ears, and my suspicious are confirmed when I see that they slope into gentle points.

"I don't...understand."

"You were attacked with black magic," the golden male says. "We're taking you to the best healer we know, but we have to go the long way."

"You still haven't explained why that is," Kent says, voice venomous and sharp.

The green male takes a step forward, "Because

traveling with magic isn't easy on your body, and if we transport her all the way there, it will kill her. Is that a good enough reason?"

Kent doesn't say anything, but he looks furious.

I swallow, and my throat is dry, but I get a few more words out. "Who are you, and where are we?"

The golden one holds the bottle to my lips again, and I let refreshing wetness soothe my throat. "My name is Brae. This is Verys," he says, pointing to my all-white angel. "And that's Aeric." The green man.

Kent looks at me. His arms are crossed like he's angry, but his eyes aren't. Not when they look at me, anyway. "We're in Allwyn."

"Oh."

It hurts too much to move, but I make my eyes focus on the scenery. This definitely isn't what I'm used to. We're in a jungle. Tall, broad trees teeming with vines and moss, the undergrowth is built up, and the very air feels green. Full of life. Streaks of sunlight shoot down from the canopy. Everything about this place screams magic, and I've always wanted to come here. I just wished it weren't like this.

The pain rises up in a wave, and I can't hold in the moan that escapes me. Nothing in my life has been like this. Not the pain in my feet after hours of pointe work. Not the broken bones I felt as a child. *Nothing.*

On the heels of the pain comes anger. Why am I here? I'm supposed to be at a gala watching my friends get the promotion of their lives. I'm supposed to be drinking and dancing with them and attempting to have fun. At least pretending that I don't desperately miss that life. The plan was not to get attacked by a blonde bitch and swept off to the faery realm. "Was the potion really that bad?"

"What?" The question comes from Verys.

I have to swallow again before I can make out the words. "I sold that fae a potion earlier today. While I was making it there was a huge burst of magic. I don't know where it came from. I offered to make her a new one, but she took it anyway."

His smile is grim. "I don't think this had anything to do with a potion."

"Then why?"

Brae is the one that speaks now. "We're going to find out. But first, we have to keep you alive."

"I'd like that." Fire slashes through me, piercing my gut and running up my spine like I've ingested live coals. I can't breathe, vision going white. There's nothing other than this, and I can taste that magic—orange and ash. It lasts forever and not at all. I don't know how long. And when it fades to a level where I can think, I realize that I'm still breathing, hauling in air. It's thick with moisture and the scent of the forest, and I cling to that. Right now, that's life.

The men—all four of them—have their eyes trained on me. They're all gorgeous, and it seems ridiculous to notice that right now. But on the bright side, if I'm going to die, at least I'll have something beautiful to look at.

My gut churns, and I roll to the side just in time to expel the water and bile that's coming up my throat. Over and over until everything that I ingested is gone. My lips burn with it, and my body is shaking now along with that ever-present ache. It's a reminder that I could be in agony at any moment.

I don't even have the strength to sit back up against the tree, I just lean to the side, avoiding my own vomit as I lay my head on the ground.

"We need to move on," Verys says, and there are murmurs of agreement from the others. Even Kent.

Hands gently turn me and lift me until I'm once again cradled in my angel's arms. Closing my eyes, I let the motion of floating rock me as we move. I can't even open my eyes.

CHAPTER FIVE

KARI

I fade in and out, floating. Ever floating. Carried by different sets of arms. I can feel the time passing, the fact that we're moving, but not much else. The backdrop is pain—rising and falling.

When I open my eyes and am suddenly clear, it feels like an electric shock. I don't know how I got here, but it's dark, and I'm leaning against another tree. This time in a clearing. Light from the fire in the center of the space is casting sinister shadows across the canopy. Beyond the edge of light, anything could be lurking. At least that's the way it feels.

Around the fire are the four men, and they're speaking. Arguing. About me. I don't think I can use my voice yet, and I can feel the agony lurking beneath my skin waiting to spike. So I close my eyes and listen. It's Kent's voice that I latch onto first.

"There has to be something that you can do."

"Not currently," Brae says softly.

Kent practically growls in frustration. "You're telling me that three powerful fae can't just use magic to make this go away?"

A third voice. Aeric, I think. "Why do you refuse to understand this? This isn't something that we can just magic away. She is *dying*. You can't just restore someone's life force."

"Just—"

"No," Brae cuts Kent off. "Aeric is correct. Just because we have magic doesn't mean we can cure her. Fae have skillsets just like humans do. For right now, the magic I'm feeding that curse, and the fact that she's on magical soil, is keeping her alive. That has to be enough until we reach Urien."

"That's taking too long," Kent says. He doesn't sound angry now. This is something else I can't identify. "If we don't—"

His voice breaks, and it sinks in what he's saying. If we don't move quickly, I'm going to die. Like I already almost died on that street in New York. Terror seeps into my chest. I don't want to die. The thought of fading into that place again makes my heart pound, and I hear myself say, "Can we portal there?"

All four of them look at me in unison, and then they're moving. Kent is by my side in seconds, and he's on his knees, looking into my eyes. There's stubble on his jaw, and I see my own terror reflected in his eyes the second before he kisses me. The gentle brush of his lips ignites butterflies in my gut, and I'm feeling a different kind of ache. No matter the gentleness, I can feel his desperation and his fear. For me.

The surge of emotion rushes through my chest, and tears fill my eyes. I've wanted Kent to kiss me for so long, and this isn't even close to how I wanted it to happen. We shouldn't be here.

The tears spill over and I can't stop them. How can I? I can barely move. But I try.

I reach out with my hand and catch his. There's so much more that I want and he understands. He's so gentle as he pulls me into his arms, and I sob against his chest. We shouldn't be here. He should be taking me to a party and pulling me away from the others to kiss me at sunset. Not while I'm dying.

I'm *dying*.

"I'm sorry," he whispers into my hair.

There's nothing that I can say back. Instead, I let the tears flow, relaxing into his body. I give in to the sadness that this isn't the way I first wanted him to hold me, or the first way I would feel his body. Kent doesn't like fae, and he's hinted that he has a very good reason for that, though we've never really talked about it. The fact that he's here with me, the fear in that kiss, the way he's holding me now say more about what he feels for me more than any words could.

It's the pain that cuts off my tears, slithering up my nerves and choking me until all I can do is breathe and dig my fingers into Kent's shirt to hold on. The only sound is the crackling flames, and I fight the urge to scream. I don't know where we are, and not all the stories about Allwyn are good ones. I have no idea if screaming is safe.

When my vision clears, I become aware of the acute silence around me—so thick that it's almost loud—with all four sets of eyes on me.

Finally, Verys speaks. "It's getting worse."

"I honestly couldn't say. It's all just pain." My voice sounds like I've run a race, jagged and rough. "But I asked before, could we portal there?"

Brae shakes his head. "We mentioned it before, last time you were awake, but I don't think you're strong enough. My gift is identifying and manipulating magic. This thing inside you—" He cuts off like he's looking for the right words. "I'm worried that it would rip you apart if we went through another portal. It's already siphoning your magic and life force somewhere else. Splitting that connection could kill you."

I swallow, noticing the way that Kent's hands tighten on me when Brae says that it might kill me. "Yeah, I'd like to avoid that."

Glancing at the other two, I realize that Aeric is staring at Kent with open hatred. Specifically, the way that Kent has his arms around me. Is holding me. I want to ask why, but I can't. The pain is rising up again, this time twisting and turning in my gut threatening to make me vomit again. I can feel myself fading again, to that floating place where nothing exists. I don't want to go back there.

"Please," I manage, and Brae is crouched in front of me.

"May I?"

I nod.

With infinite gentleness, he places his hand on my chest. It feels like a streak of pure sunlight is being poured into my heart. Shimmering heat and brilliance, and the pain eases, leaving my body limp in Kent's arms. But I can't look away from Brae, and his golden brown eyes are fixed on mine as he pours more of his magic into my body until I'm bathed in it. The sensation is like being encased in golden light, and for a brief moment, I can't feel the pain slithering under my skin.

I smile at him, even though that motion feels foreign to me right now. "Thank you."

"You're very welcome, Kari," he says softly, his hand still on my chest.

There's a flutter in my gut, and I look away, suddenly aware of how I'm in Kent's arms. Brae pulls his hand from my skin, and as soon as he does, I'm exhausted. The pain is gone, but all I want to do is sleep. My eyes are already closing.

"How long until we can reach your friend?" Kent asks.

Verys sighs, "If all goes well, a week."

"That's a long time."

"It is," Brae agrees, "But if she can continue to survive on our magic, all will be well."

Aeric clears his throat. "We can take tonight though. For her to rest."

There are sounds of agreement and shuffling as they move. I don't have my eyes open anymore, and I don't think that I can keep myself upright.

"Kari," Kent whispers in my ear. "Can I stay with you?"

I'm too tired to do anything but nod once. He takes over, lowering me to the ground so I'm pillowed on his arm, and holding me close. "Sleep," he says, his lips pressing to my temple. "I've got you."

CHAPTER SIX

KENT

I watch Kari fade into sleep, and sweet, pure relief flows through me as her body relaxes. I've never been as fucking terrified as I am right now, but I'm sure as hell not going to let those fae bastards see it. The past year seems like a blur, and I've been reliving every time I could have kissed her, but didn't. Every time I could have asked her out and acted on the feelings that we both knew we had.

Instead, I'm here. In Allwyn. I swore never to set foot in Allwyn again and I do my damnedest every day to track down the terrible things that leak from here into the human world. But for Kari, I'd do it a thousand times. I will do it a thousand more times if it means that she survives.

Seeing her writhe in pain and not being able to

do anything about it—the anger that rises in my chest is enough to make me feel like I can set something on fire. Twelve hours ago I thought that we were finally going to be together. This isn't what I meant. I've been in love with her for what seems like forever, and I'm sure as hell not ready to let her go yet. I'm not going to let another person that I love be taken away by the fucking fae.

I swear if that happens, I'll burn it all to the fucking ground.

The anger in my chest is oppressive, and I need to move. Need to breathe. I move slowly so that I don't disturb Kari. She needs every bit of pain-free rest that she can get, and I'm not going to get in the way of that. But as soon as she's laying peacefully, I make a beeline for the trees and step outside the ring of light.

We're in a fucking jungle. Part of the Kingdom of Nature, or so I was told by the pale one—Verys. All I know is that it's vividly bright and humid and there are too many hiding places to make me feel truly comfortable. In the night, the humidity has condensed into mist, making the spaces between the trees milky. The light from the fire spears outward into the night like a beacon. The only thing keeping me from putting it out is the idea that we might be more vulnerable without it.

I pace back and forth between two large trees, moving as fast as I can without breaking into a run. There's an itch to jump and scream, and I just need to take the edge off with some kind of movement. If I were home I'd put on my gloves and beat the hell out of a bag, but I don't think my hands would appreciate me beating the hell out of this tree. I need more than this, or I'm going to explode.

The sense of movement is there more than any sound, and I turn to find Aeric watching me. Sneaky bastards, the fae. I hate that they can move so silently. "Shouldn't sneak up on people," I say. "Could get a fist to the face."

Aeric smirks. "You wouldn't be able to hit me."

"Care to back that up?" I'm itching for a fight, and more than anything he's the one I want to do it with. The way he's been staring at me makes it clear that he's not a fan. Well, the feeling is mutual.

"That's not an effective use of my time," Aeric says. "But after this is over, if you still want a beating, I'll happily give you one."

"We'll see about that," I mutter.

He leans against the tree. "Why are you away from Kari? It seemed like you couldn't wait to get your hands on her."

I start to pace again, trying to ignore his question. It's none of his business, but at the same time I find myself answering. "I was angry enough that I was afraid that I would wake her. And once she's safe and home, I'm going to prove that you all did this. After that, it'll be open season on the three of you. Not even fae laws will save you, and I will find you."

Aeric laughs, but it's a humorless sound. "Be my guest, Williams. If you'd gotten there five minutes earlier, you'd have all the proof that you need to know that we didn't do this. And if we did, why would we be going to all this trouble to save her?" He pushes himself off the trunk and takes a step towards me. "None of us want her to die. Don't you get that? That's the *last thing* any of us want."

There's an unmistakable sound of bitterness in his words, but they can't be a lie. I can feel the truth in them. But there's still that nagging voice in the back of my head. Fae don't take an interest in humans for no reason. There has to be something about Kari that drew them to her. And I'm still not convinced they didn't do this—that it wasn't a set-up to get Kari into Allwyn. And besides. All that stuff about fae not being able to lie is bullshit.

"Why?" I ask.

"Why what?"

I clear my throat. "Why don't you want her to die? She's a human. She's nothing to you. She's—"

Aeric moves past me, cutting so close I nearly lose my balance stepping out of the way. He mutters something about keeping watch, but doesn't turn around as he disappears into the halo of firelight. Shit.

Should have known better than to expect information from a fae.

The rabid energy is still running through my body, and I can't get the feeling out. I wish I were far from here, where I could run and rage and a hundred other things. But then Kari would be here alone. With them.

I drop to the ground and start to do pushups. Then crunches. Then burpees. It still isn't enough. But now I'm sweating, and there's no way that I'm going to be able to rid myself of this feeling. Not tonight. I'm going to have to swallow it and try to breathe. For Kari.

Stepping back inside the ring on firelight, my eyes go straight to her. Aeric is on the other side of the clearing, back to me. Good.

Kari hasn't moved from where I left her, though she looks paler. Somehow less vibrant, like some of the color has been stolen from her hair and skin. But she's still beautiful. She'll always be beautiful. It feels impossible to want someone so much. I swear, I've never felt about anyone the way I've felt about her. For a brief second, my mind flips to the fantasies that I've had about her—about what would happen when I eventually took her to bed.

Within seconds I'm hard, and I curse myself because how fucked up do I have to be to want her like this? When she's dying and in pain?

But it doesn't matter. I'll always want Kari. In any state. Forever.

I lie down next to her and hold her as tightly as I dare, but it's a long time before I'm able to sink into sleep.

CHAPTER SEVEN

AERIC

I wait until I hear the humans' breath smooth out with sleep before I speak. "I know that you're awake."

Brae and Verys rise with barely a whisper of sound and join me at the edge of the clearing. This is the first time that we've been remotely alone since this happened, and all of us should rest, but like them, I don't think that I could close my eyes. I'm swirling inside with the pull toward Kari, what it means, and how much I don't want this to be happening right now.

"This can't be an accident," Verys says.

"The fact that we were there?"

He nods. "I have no idea if any other fae were close enough to feel what we felt, or to save her. But it feels…"

"Important," Brae finishes for him. "I know. Even without everything else, the Goddess wants her alive."

I bristle a little, muscles tensing. No. I throw my senses outward, listening to the jungle for any sign that we've been followed, letting the rich scent of nature speak to me and calm my mind. Even from here I can catch her scent, sweet sugar and roses. Perfect and delicate. Sorting out my senses grounds me, and I'm able to bring my focus back to Brae. It's not his fault that this is the last thing that I want, or the fact that any time someone tells me something is willed by the Goddess I want to scream and hit something. I've had too many people justify bad things with that excuse. But in this case, he might be right.

It doesn't make me feel better.

"So you both?" I ask. There's no need to tell them what I'm referring to. It's like a tug in my gut, leading straight to Kari. The three of us felt a pulse of magic when we exited into the human world, and now I know what it was. But I don't want it. Not like this.

Please, I pray, hoping that she'll hear me and listen even through my anger. *Please, not like this*.

"Yes," Brae says. "It's how I know that it can't

be an accident. There aren't coincidences like that in Allwyn."

Verys nods too.

"But we weren't in Allwyn," I protest. "We were in fucking New York."

Brae gives me a look that I deserve, because even I'm not that stupid. "How long ago were we invited to that performance? How much time did Kallan spend in the human world preparing? How—"

I cut him off with a raised hand. "I know. I just—this isn't what I had planned."

Verys smiles grimly. "In my experience, what you have planned and what the Goddess has planned for you are rarely the same."

I swallow down the words that are about to fly from my lips, because if anyone would know, it's Verys. "Well," I say, "I want to be sure. When we cross the border, we'll know."

"Yes," Brae says with a sigh. "Though I'm not sure I need that to know."

I grit my teeth and resist responding. Glancing out into the woods, I scan the mist that's seeping through the trees. All of it seems to be quiet, for now, even though we're broadcasting our presence with the firelight. This section of the Kingdom of

Nature isn't one where I'd expect to encounter much danger—unless we've been followed.

"We need to move faster," I say.

"Do you think she can ride?" Verys asks, the question directed at Brae.

He nods. "Yes, but not on her own. It'll have to be one of us."

"Not with him," I say, nodding to where Kari and Kent are tangled in sleep. His hands are possessive, even unconscious, curling around her hips and back. The urge to walk over and tear them off rises, but I don't want to wake her. Seeing her in pain sends terror twisting through my gut, and the fact that she has some peace on her face is comforting. For now.

That dress she's wearing, dirty and tattered from our travel, still clings to her body in a way that I can't look away from. My eyes seek out the places that her pale skin is exposed, and my anger flares again at the human man because right now, I'd do almost anything to take his place.

Verys makes a non-committal sound. "He knows her, and he clearly cares about her. We're strangers. If she wants to ride with him, we can't stop that."

"He's still human," I say. "He can't carry her as long as we can."

"A point that I'm sure will make him like us that

much more," Brae says with a wince. "I heard your conversation."

A soft breeze picks up through the trees, unsettling the mist and sending tendrils of it towards the fire like a cold hand reaching. "Don't worry about it. As long as we keep her alive, he can't hurt us." I swallow, the next words painful as I speak them. "Even if she doesn't survive, he won't be a problem."

I hear Brae's sudden intake of breath, and Verys goes very still. The thought of Kari dying, even the possibility, feels like a hole is opening up in the earth beneath me. A giant fist is clutching tight around my chest and I can't breathe.

"We'll get her to Urien," Brae says. "If anyone can break a curse like this, it's him."

"Do you have enough magic to keep her alive until then?"

He shakes his head. "Maybe. I'll have to recover some at some point. Or she might be able to use it, if it's combined."

Verys snorts. "That ought to go over well with Kent."

Looking over at Kari again, she looks even more pale. The life is being leeched from her before our eyes, and only the thin barrier of Brae's magic is stopping it. "He'll like what keeps her alive. You can have whatever magic you need from me," I say.

"Mine too," Verys says.

He's staring at her too. She's leaned back, her arm fallen out of Kent's embrace. It looks like she's reaching towards the fire. Towards warmth and light and life. Everything about her speaks to me. I want to *know* her. I want to touch her. I want to do everything to her and with her.

Shit.

Brae is right, I don't need to get to the border to know.

I push that thought aside, because I can't think about it. All I can think about is making sure that Kari stays alive. Everything else has to wait.

"Let's get some rest," I say. "We should move as soon as day breaks."

CHAPTER EIGHT

KARI

I wake with a start and the sensation that I'm falling, but I'm not. Just moving. But this motion is different, and the world is coming to me in pieces.

The pain today is an ache that's attached to my bones. I want to scratch at it, rip it out of my limbs and gut, but when I move my fingers they barely flicker. I'm cold too, but I'm pressed against warmth and it feels good.

"Welcome back to the world." The voice vibrates through me. That piece hadn't hit me yet. There's an arm around my waist and I'm sitting upright, pulled close to his body.

As I open my eyes, there's green everywhere — sun shining through the trees and mist, lighting up the space around us like an emerald and reflecting against Aeric's already green hair and skin.

"Hi," I say. It's quiet. My throat is dry and it's all I can manage, but I see the side of his mouth turn up into a small smile and I know that he doesn't mind.

It's a strange angle to look at someone's face, leaning against his shoulder the way I am. But he has a beautiful profile, and I get a gorgeous look at his jaw. I used to laugh when people used the expression that a jaw could 'cut glass.'

Now I know what they meant.

Aeric is the source of the warmth I feel, and right now I don't ever want to move away. It feels like he's a fire and that I've just come in from the cold. I would blush—if my body were capable of it right now—because all I want to do is snuggle closer to him. He's Fae and gorgeous and so far out of my league that it's silly. Not to mention that the fact that I'm even thinking about that right now feels wrong.

As if he's reading my thoughts, Aeric looks down at me. I don't think that I've ever seen eyes this color green. It's a true and pure green. *Vivid*. Darker than his skin, but lighter and brighter than his hair. They're captivating. But right now they're assessing me. "Are you all right?"

"I think so."

"The pain?"

I sigh, relaxing my body further against his, because just the reminder of it makes me tired. "That's always there."

It occurs to me that the thing that woke me was the sensation of movement, but Aeric isn't carrying me. We're riding. With an effort, I sit up, and Aeric's arm on my back supports me. Amazingly, I feel solid in the motion, like he's lending me magical strength. I suppose it's possible that he is.

My legs are slung across his, and we're both on…a horse? But it doesn't look like any horse that I've ever seen. If not for the familiar shape, it would seem like we're riding a tree or a bush. In front of us, Kent rides a similar creature, and I can get a better look.

The tail I see is formed of hanging vines, its body from moss, bark, leaves, and what looks like jasmine flowers.

"What is it?"

Aeric props me up more in his arms, my back leaning against his chest, and his lips are close to my ear. He doesn't speak loudly. "A fae beast. Humans might call them elementals. These will take the shape you need if they're in a good mood and you make a good bargain with them."

"I had kind of hoped that fae horses were like this," I say. "It seems more magical that way."

I slip a little, and his hand grows tighter around my waist. "Fae horses are beautiful too," he says. "Born in every color that you can imagine, but they are horses. We'll have to make sure you see some."

Sadness wells in my chest like a wave, and I fight the rise of tears. I turn my head slowly, looking at our surroundings. It's beautiful. Otherworldly, because this is a jungle, and yet it's not. Not in a way that I've ever seen. The air is richer here, the mist swirling through the trees and spilling rainbows over everything as the sun refracts through it. Vines cover the trees and hang from the branches, holding flowers that are bigger than I've ever seen in shades of color so bright that I'm pretty sure I'm hallucinating.

Sounds float through the air too, songs from birds that I can't see. Melodies that could be in a symphony, other birds harmonizing with them. Everything feels so very *alive*. Except for me. I'm the only thing in Allwyn that's dying. It's stunning, and I won't be able to enjoy it. The world blurs through my tears, and I duck my head. "I always wanted to come here," I say. "I've wanted to see Allwyn forever. I never thought it would be like this."

I feel Aeric's body go incredibly still next to mine. "What do you mean?"

It takes a moment to find the right words, and I swallow. "I wanted to come here and explore, but I never thought it would be the last thing I saw before I died."

Aeric turns my body towards him, still holding me close, and then his hand is under my chin, raising my gaze so it's locked with his. "We are not bringing you all the way across the Kingdoms just to put you in a grave." His fingers tighten on my hip, and I'm very aware of how close we are together, how I can feel his body under mine while he has me pinned with that emerald gaze. I can't look away. "I'm not going to let you die. Do you understand?"

The certainty in his voice is a command, combined with a genuine certainty that I can feel down in my gut. His words make me feel safe. He's not going to let it happen, and I believe him. "Yes." The way we're so close feels like we could close the gap—like he could lean down and kiss me at any second. Aeric's eyes flicker to my lips, and for a moment I think that he's going to do it. I hold my breath, because I'm not sure what will happen if he does. Do I want him to? My gut says yes and no and yes again, and then he's pulling away and the spell is broken.

"Good," He says, and I find myself able to breathe again.

Suddenly Kent is by our side. We'd been talking in whispers before, but Aeric abandoned that just now. Everyone knows that I'm awake.

Kent's eyes roam over my body, filled with concern. "Kari?"

I can hear the question in his voice. Am I all right? Am I safe? There's more there too, the way his eyes linger on me and my memory of the way he held me as I slept that makes me warm, and the fact that I was a breath away from kissing Aeric. I can feel my body trying to blush, I'm glad that it seems like I can't. "I'm okay." I give him a smile, hoping that it gives him some comfort.

He nods, and returns to his place in front of us. The look that he gives Aeric isn't friendly. When he's once again out of earshot, Aeric says, "You can ride with him if you like." The tone he uses is carefully neutral, and my attention is drawn to his hand on my waist as he grips me a fraction tighter.

Riding with Kent would be wonderful. I'm probably never going to admit the number of times I've dreamt about being in his arms. But the thought of moving right now, when Aeric is so warm, is exhausting. I feel guilty for not wanting to go with

Kent, but I'm enjoying this. "I don't want to move," I say softly.

"Very well."

I must be imagining the tone of satisfaction in his voice.

"Where are we?"

He looks around, taking in the jungle that we're passing. "We're in the Kingdom of Flora, close to the Court of the Rainforest."

Pain surges in my arms and my legs, and I gasp. No. I won't do this. I'm not going to be a victim to this. Distraction. I need distraction, so I keep going even though I feel him watching me now. "I had no idea that that court existed."

"Allwyn is much more complex than humans know. There are hundreds of courts, if not more. Some are as small as only one person. Some contain thousands. But we have Kingdoms too. Those courts with similarities are often close. Though it's not always that way."

"We will see the rainforest court?" I ask through gritted teeth. The pain is pulsing now, seeming to spread the intensity with each one of my heartbeats.

"No," Aeric says, "I don't think so. It's out of the way, and we're making better time with the mounts."

I have to close my eyes. I listen to the sound of

his heart under my ear, and the steady sound gives me focus. Feeling his breath calms me down. I can do this. "So where are we going?"

It takes me a second to realize that Aeric has stopped our mount, and a glance forward tells me Brae has stopped his too. Chills prickle across my skin like a warning. The trees around us have gone eerily silent. No more symphony. There's not even any rustling leaves or branches. It's like the entire jungle has taken a breath and held it.

"Aeric—"

He puts a finger to my lips to indicate silence.

Something is very wrong.

All at once Aeric has me in his arms and we're off the mount and on the ground. Verys and Brae appear next to us, and the fae beasts are nowhere to be seen. Aeric places me on my feet, but my legs buckle, and Kent catches me before I hit the ground. I *hate* this. I hate being this helpless. Bright red anger washes through me and gives me enough strength to stand. But barely. The pain is pounding so hard now that I'm squinting through it. I will not fall. I will. Not. Fall.

"What's going on?" Kent hisses, and Brae nods his head in the direction we came from.

I follow his gaze, and my stomach drops. Creeping through the trees in a different kind of mist—a thick fog that I can see rolling, crawling across the ground and over the underbrush. It shines with a sickly yellow light, barring any doubt that it's not a natural phenomenon.

The three fae position themselves around us. "Keep her on her feet," Aeric says. "We need to move."

Kent bristles at the tone, but he wraps his arm around me, taking most of my weight. Without him, I doubt I'd be able to lift my feet.

Before we can take a step, a shriek sounds through the trees. It's not human. A bird, maybe. But like no bird I've ever heard. Another cry, this one a low and raucous caw. And another, a series of shrill tones rising one over the other.

"There." Verys points to a branch where a bird sits.

It's a massive raven, or might look like one if it weren't the same sickly yellow as that fog. There's another one in the tree beyond it, and I spy a third one too. The branches all around us are filled with birds, more appearing every second. The air is filled with nightmarish sound.

I jump at the heavy thud of impact, losing my balance, and turn far enough to see that one of the birds falling away from Aeric. Another one dives towards us and slams into an invisible wall in front of Verys. There's a burst of light when the bird strikes that wall, and it strikes me. Magic. They're holding magic around us, protecting us.

The forest goes silent again, and I shiver. I feel the weight of attention as all the birds look towards us in unison. We're being hunted.

"Go," Brae says. "Now."

We start to move, as fast as we can, working through the underbrush and around the trees, trying to travel as a unit. I can't move fast even with Kent supporting me. Every step I take is like walking on daggers.

The fog is faster, seeping up around us, catching at our heels. It burns, little drops of fire when the moisture meets my skin. Shit. Kent pulls me down and a blast of air rushes past me along with a shriek as one of the ravens falls on us from above. Slamming into the ground is like feeling all my bones break, but he has me up on my feet again, pulling me along.

For a second I manage to look back the way we came, and it's a wall of fog. The jungle fades away behind us into opaque yellow air. Everything is being swallowed by it. And the trees are swarming. Every branch on every tree is covered in ravens, all of them staring at us. One after another diving after us, only to be repelled by magic. But there's more diving at once.

Kent pulls me forward, but I can't look away. Beyond the trees is a figure, hooded, shrouded in the fog. There's more than one, and they're everywhere I look, following. It's her. It has to be her. I can't see clearly enough to know for sure, but I feel it.

My heart is pounding in my ears, and the trees are echoing with the raw shrieks of the poisonous birds. They slam against the fae shields in waves, the sound of them striking it almost as loud as their screams. I stumble over the root of a tree and Kent catches me a split second before I go down. "I can't," I tell him. My legs about to give out, and we need to go faster.

"I've got you." He scoops me into his arms without hesitation and I let him carry me. The sky is a flurry of wings and screams, and we're running now. I'm shaking, adrenaline spinning through my limbs as we run. The only sound is the sound of the birds and them falling away. Brae grunts in effort as a rush of ravens collide with his magic. He cuts down a bird out of the air with a sword, and it dissolves into mist.

They all have swords. Where did they get swords?

They're cutting through the birds and holding the majority of them back. But there's so many. Too many. I see one swoop over Verys and narrowly avoid a swing from his sword. I can't yell out in warning before it collides with Kent from behind. We stumble together and he recovers at the last second, the raven exploding into poisonous, burning, fog under Verys's sword.

Talons rip into my shoulder, and I'm thrown back to that moment in the street. I'm on the ground and I'm dying. Bitter, rotten orange floods my senses, pulling my life away like sand is pouring out of an hourglass. Beak and claws rip my skin, and this is the end. I can feel it coming. She's here. She found me. There's a chance that I'm screaming, but I can't hear it.

Foul-smelling mist explodes across my face and the bird evaporates. "Go!" Brae roars over the noise of the birds. And it feels like we're flying. My skin is searing, blistering, raging from the fog that's overtaking us. The figures in the mist are getting closer. I can barely see them through the storm of ravens.

The air around us smells stale and acrid. If the trees of the jungle weren't around me, I would think that we were on the slopes of a volcano. The world feels like it's slipping, turning on its side. Kent's voice is vibrating in my chest, speaking words that I can't understand. I can feel the magic in my chest and somewhere I can feel the fresh air that I can suddenly breathe, but the fog hasn't left my mind.

I'm going to disappear into it, following the figures into the trees. I can hear their voices trying to call me back.

CHAPTER NINE

KARI

Sometimes pain is a color. Sometimes it's a lens. It's filtering everything that I see, highlighting some things, washing others away. The jungle is long gone, eclipsed by trees and mounds of stone and crystal, swirling shapes that shouldn't exist in substances this hard. I think I catch a glimpse of mountains in the distance, but I'm not sure, my eyes won't focus on the horizon.

The waves of agony start in my shoulder, falling down through my chest—which feels like it's cracking—and shimmering down through the rest of me, aching and twisting. This pain makes me want to writhe, try to find a position that hurts less, to move and try to outrun it. I don't have the strength to do either.

There's a tree—but it's not a tree. It's a spire of

white stone resembling a pine down to the needles. It sounds like a wind chime as we pass it. I'm alive. I'm not sure how.

"There!" a voice calls, and the body supporting mine changes direction. Dizziness spirals through my mind and everything goes black for a second. I open my eyes again and see an impossibly big crystal above me. Will it fall? No. It doesn't seem to be moving. I'm moving. There's more rock and crystal overhead, and the whispers from the men around me have started to echo.

I'm laid against something hard, the surface behind me keeping me upright. We're in a cave. It looks like a geode, with glassy purple fragments jutting out from the walls in unpredictable patterns. They're lit from the entrance of the cave with watery daylight that turns to brilliance as Verys points to the ground and fire erupts.

I have to close my eyes against the sudden shimmer, but when they adjust, it's beautiful. In any other circumstance, I would be in awe. Trying to find my focus, I look at the men's faces. Brae is closest to me, lips pressed into a line, but his eyes are darting over me. Like he's looking for further signs of the attack. He looks tired—his golden skin a little paler than before—and he's breathing harder than I've seen. His clothes are ripped, and I can see bloody scratches on his shoulders. Everyone has injuries that they're ignoring.

The look on Brae's face is mirrored on Aeric's as he turns and stands in the entrance of the cave, keeping watch. And on Verys's as he finishes a twist with his hand, molding the fire so it doesn't escape his hold. I'm not sure how I know that's what he's doing, but I do. I look at him again, and he meets my eyes. Panic. That's what they're hiding. Panic for me or that we're going to be attacked again, I'm not sure.

Kent isn't hiding anything—he's pacing back and forth in the cave, hands running through his hair. When he looks at me, his eyes are wild. Pushing out a breath, he comes over to me, placing a hand over my injured shoulder. The pain is suddenly blistering fire and he pulls away at my gasp.

It's like all the air has been sucked out of the world. Not just for me, but when I look at them. I manage to take a breath, and I'm so tired. I could just go to sleep right here. Deep in my gut, I know that I shouldn't. I pull what energy I have left up and form the words. "What aren't you saying?" I ask, directing the question at anyone who will answer.

"The magic is the same but different. When we

brought you across the veil, the fact that you were in Allwyn gave you a small measure of protection. Magic can be tied to a place, and that was deeply tied to the human world, *preying* on the fact that you were human. But this time it's not. Being here won't protect you against it, and it's moving much faster. It's feeding off your life force." Brae finishes his explanation.

Kent is up and moving again, like the energy inside him will not allow him to stay still. "So give her more magic. It's been working up till now. Why is it different?"

"It's going to consume it much faster now," he says, "and she needs more than I have."

"It's magic," Kent says, stopping to glare at Brae. "You're saying that you can run out?"

Verys's voice cuts in, soft and level. "A lot of what humans are taught about magic is wrong. It's not infinite. If we use too much, we have to let it recharge, much like using physical energy. We can create more, but…"

He trails off into silence, and the three fae share looks. They seem impossibly uncomfortable, and I didn't think it could happen to fae, but they look awkward.

"What?" Kent asks, and I'm glad that he does.

"It's not that simple," Verys says.

Aeric stiffens and turns away again as Brae clears his throat. "All fae have magic that stems from Allwyn itself, our gift from the Goddess. It's a relatively small piece that's always with us. The rest comes from our Kingdom and Court alignment, which is passed through lineage or sometimes chosen by the Goddess.

"When we're at home, we have access to all the magic we could need. We can raise as much as we like—a nearly infinite supply—because that's our home, and the land is steeped in *our* magic. It's not the same in the other Kingdoms."

"So you could raise more?" I ask.

Brae nods, but says nothing more.

The anger in Kent's tone is starting to overflow. "There's something you're still not telling us."

Verys and Brae share a look before Brae speaks again. "We're members of the Carnal Court."

The words feel full, like they have more substance than other words. Almost as if Brae is invoking something powerful. "The Carnal Court?" I echo.

They share a look again, but don't speak. It's Aeric who turns around, exasperated. "Our magic flows from acts of physical pleasure and sex."

His eyes connect with mine, and he smiles. It's just a small one, but it has me remembering riding with him on that horse, supported by his body and the delicious strength that it has. I blush, and even that hurts. Though it's something that I can do even that right now. The smirk fades off of his face as he turns away again, troubled.

"What does that mean?" Kent asks. "You have to go jerk off to get more magic?"

I give him a look and he backs down, raising his hand in apology. They're trying to help, and I'm not going to let him constantly fight. Even though I don't really have the strength to stop him.

In spite of Kent's tone, Brae laughs a little. "That would give me more to work with, but it wouldn't help Kari."

Verys cuts in, "That's the other thing about magic. It's most effective when used in combination with our alignment. For example, a Fae of the water kingdom will always be able to heal someone more effectively if they can use water to conduct the magic."

Kent is staring at Verys, and I can tell that he doesn't get it. I've made the leap, and look at Brae. He nods slightly, and I blush again.

"So no matter how much magic I feed Kari," Brae says, clearing his throat again and holding my gaze, "It won't be any more effective unless she's receiving physical pleasure."

God, my mind is suddenly filled with images of sex. With Kent. With all of them. Even if I am dying I'm not fucking blind, and I'm sure that being with any of them would give me more than enough pleasure for this to work. My blood warms under the pain, and I keep myself still, not giving any indication that my body is reacting to the idea. Because that's not going to happen, even if my body impossibly wants that. Any of it. All of it. I'm blushing again, trying to shove the images of hard fae bodies out of my mind.

Kent's voice explodes through the cave, "If you so much as lay a hand on her—"

"I didn't say that it couldn't be self-pleasure," Brae says quickly, raising his hands like he's surrendering. "But if my magic—any of our magic—is going to have a chance at slowing this down, it has to be that."

The pain has slowly morphed from the twisting ache back into that feeling of burning acid, but still, I'm suddenly laughing. The irony of this isn't lost on me, and they all look at me like I'm crazy. Even Aeric, which just makes me laugh harder, even though it hurts. "You're telling me that in order to stop this I have to masturbate."

The fae nod, and Kent looks a little embarrassed.

"If I don't masturbate, I'm going to die."

Brae nods.

I shake my head, fighting the giggles bubbling through my lips. "Of course I'll do it. Even if it is the last thing I thought you were going to say. I'll do anything to make it stop." A flare of fire lances through my chest, and my voice rasps into nothing.

The air goes tense and still again. Brae looks at Verys. "We need food."

He nods, standing up from his place by the fire and grabbing Kent by the arm. "We'll find some."

Aeric grabs Kent's other arm, even though he's struggling. "I'm not leaving her alone with him—"

Brae cuts Kent's words off again as he stands. It's becoming a habit. "I will give Kari what magic I can and then keep watch outside of the cave so she can have some privacy. Just as you should, by leaving."

His words are flat and final, and Kent looks to me, the question in his eyes. Will I be all right?

I nod, and he stops struggling. It's not the answer that I think he wanted, but I trust Brae. He's not going to hurt me, and if I can feel better, then I'm going to do it. I don't care. I'm sick of the pain.

Kent doesn't stop looking at me until he's out of sight, disappearing behind a strange formation of blue and orange rock that looks like cubes within cubes.

And then I'm alone with Brae, and I'm very aware that I'm still in my grey dress, though now it's ripped to shreds and frankly exposes more than it hides. Blood stains the top of it from the bird that attacked my shoulder, but I look at it, and the skin is healed over—likely a side effect from the magic Brae used to keep me alive. The fabric is thin, and everything about my body is completely obvious. I can't help but think about it, because of what I'm about to do, and also the fact that Brae might as well be a Greek god of perfection.

He smiles, but his eyes are sad as he leans down and gently places his hand on my stomach. "I'm sorry about this."

I laugh, though it doesn't seem very funny. "I never thought that masturbating would save my life."

He laughs too, and I feel that warm, sunny glow of magic seeping into my skin. The magic gives off a scent that's like him, honey and nutty. It reminds me of toasted chestnuts at Christmas time.

Even just the magic does make me feel a little better, but he's right, it doesn't have the same effect it did before the attack. The fog and the birds. "I'll be outside. If you call me, I will hear you."

"Thank you."

He's looking into my eyes, and his hand is still

on me even though he's not passing magic anymore, and I'm finding it hard to look away. But I'm finally the one that breaks the gaze. His hand lingers for a second longer, and I miss the heat his fingers offered when he pulls away. I watch him disappear into the maze of stone outside.

It's the first time I've been completely alone since the first attack, and I take a shuddering breath. She's not here. Brae is watching. I am safe.

I can feel the magic stirring under my skin, and I need to use it. Slowly, moving past the pain, I pull my dress up past my thighs, bunching it around my hips. I didn't wear underwear that night because I didn't want to ruin the line of the dress even with a thong. And part of me was considering leaving the party early and calling Kent. If only that was the way it had gone, I wouldn't be on the floor of a crystal cave trying to pleasure myself back to life.

A little laugh hiccups in my chest. This is…I don't know what this is. Impossible. The last thing that I ever imagined.

Conjuring up the image of Kent, I try to recall one of the fantasies that I'd created for myself back in New York when life was normal and everything seemed simple. I wanted him to come into the shop just as I was closing so it was just the two of us, and he wouldn't give me a chance to say anything, just kiss me. I wanted him to push me up against the cabinets with all my ingredients and not care about the damage that he did. His kiss would be raw and fiery, and neither of us would be able to wait to get to his place or mine. I imagine him pulling me into the back room, and that's where I usually let the fantasy truly unfurl into heat and skin and lips and *god, yes*.

Touching myself isn't sexy right now. I'm wet, but just barely, and there's no spark of excitement behind my touch. I feel blank even though I'm playing the familiar images of Kent slowly stripping me down, using his mouth to explore every new bit of my body before he takes me. My body doesn't respond the way it usually does—the way it should or the way I want it to. I know that this needs to happen. It's life or death. And that's in my head.

Being alone in this cave is terrifying. The reflections from the fire are dancing across the crystal facets creating shadows and phantoms that keep jumping in the corners of my vision. That taste of rotten citrus is rolling across my tongue and images of fog and birds and cruel eyes push out the vision of Kent and our sexy time.

Closing my eyes, I force myself to focus. I can do this. I know how to make myself feel good. I rub circles around my clit, spreading the small bit of moisture across it so there's smooth friction. And it does feel good. But I'm kidding myself if I think it's going anywhere.

I think of Aeric and Brae. Verys too. They're distractingly hot. Delicious. And I've had more than one moment with them where I felt like something was about to happen between us. But I can't even get far enough to imagine them taking off their clothes, a spike of pain lancing up my spine and rendering me breathless.

But I still try. I try, and I try, and I try. Until my hand is tired. Until I'm remembering past orgasms trying to get my body to do *something*. But nothing is working, and now all I feel is dizzy and that burning agony sizzling in my nerves. Sweat covers my skin and I'm sagging against the wall of the cave. It's the only thing still holding me upright.

I don't think I can do this. Sudden tears blur my vision. I can't even do this. The one thing I should be able to do to help myself, and I can't. I've always hated feeling helpless, and this above and beyond anything I thought I could experience. The feeling is sharp between my ribs — the final blow.

But I can't let this be the thing that stands between me living and dying. A tear spills over, and I'm already flushed with embarrassment. I can't believe that I'm going to do this. My mind spins through every possibility. Anything.

But there's nothing left.

"Brae." My voice is barely a whisper.

He appears the way he left, coming around a twisting pillar of stone, and his eyes take in all of me: my state of disarray and the fact that I'm obviously not any better. "Are you all right?"

I shake my head no. My body is burning with embarrassment now, heat and pain combined make me close my eyes. I turn my face away so he can't see the tears that have fallen. I can't look at him when I ask this. "Help me," I say. "I can't."

There's a space of silence so complete I have to look back to make sure that he's still there. He is, looking at me again, but his gaze is different now.

I watch as his eyes go dark. There's no chance that he misunderstands what I'm saying, and he takes a step forward. Then he pauses. "Are you sure?"

No. Because there's something deep in my gut that tells me that this is going to change everything. But out loud, I say, "Please."

It's my only pleading prayer.

He kneels beside me, and his hand finds that place, low on my belly, where it rested before, and the magic he gave me stirs at his touch, swirling light. I can't ignore the fact that he's beautiful, and I am attracted to him. Who wouldn't be? I feel drawn to him, even though we barely know each other. But he's been saving my life from the second we met, and he didn't say no. He only asked me if I was sure. Is it possible he wants this too?

The thought makes my brain stutter. That I want this beyond just the practical, and he's there with me. Oh my god. I can't believe that I'm doing this. That I asked for this. That he's going to touch me. I want him to touch me. But that doesn't stop my skin from flushing.

He speaks again, drawing my attention back. "Why are you crying?"

I do my best to swipe the tears away. It doesn't work that well. The embarrassment wells in my throat and it takes me a moment to speak. "I'm…" More tears spill over. "I'm so embarrassed."

"Don't be." His tone is gentle but firm. "Don't ever be embarrassed about asking for what you want or need." Ever so slightly, his fingers move across the silk of my dress. There's so little separating him from my skin. It's basically nothing. "But Kari, this isn't something that we take lightly," he says. "I don't want there to be any question."

I'm looking into his eyes. They're dark and clear, and asking me to be certain, but I don't see any other hesitation from him. It's down to me. And yes, I want this. I need it. "I'm sure," I breathe. "Help me. Please."

Brae's hand cups the back of my neck, tilting my face to his, and his mouth covers mine. This kiss is soft and slow, but deliberate. Little bits of magic fly up through my body to meet him, and my lips tingle and fizz with it. It tastes like honey. Or maybe that's him. His tongue grazes my lips, and I open to him with a gasp.

Electricity hums through me, my whole body coming to attention. This isn't like any kiss I've ever had. It's more, somehow. Exquisite, and now I'm a different kind of dizzy. How do I feel like this just from a kiss? How can I feel like this even when my body is thrumming with pain?

I'm kissing a fae. A stunning, powerful fae whose very essence comes from sex. I feel like an idiot for not putting two and two together. No one could be as beautiful as these males are and not be living gods of pleasure.

My body is on more familiar ground now, reacting to Brae's kiss. Goosebumps roll across my skin and my nipples harden through the thin fabric of my dress. I'm already wetter than I was touching myself, and it's just his lips. And tongue. God, I'm imagining what he could do with his tongue as it dances with mine, and it's making me blush.

Brae's free hand drifts from my stomach lower, grazing my exposed thigh before moving upward again. His fingers barely brush my skin, teasing me as his hand disappears beneath my dress. I can feel the magic move lower, warming me with heat and arousal as he guides it. My pain recedes a little, and I'm filled with a new, different ache.

He breaks the kiss but doesn't move, keeping our gazes locked together. When he touches me for the first time, he's watching me. It's barely a touch, just a brush across my clit, but I shudder. Slow circles, gentle at first and getting firmer. I relax into his touch, not even realizing that I had tensed. But this…this feels good.

Magic swirls under my skin, sending a pulse of pleasure through me, and I let out a slow breath. It's going to work. This is going somewhere. Fingers tease downwards until they find my entrance, and the hand on my neck grips me a little harder as he slips a finger inside. I'm so wet now that he goes in easily, and I have to close my eyes.

Brae's fingers are long, and he doesn't even have to stretch to brush that spot inside that makes me shake with pleasure. It sends sparkles across the darkness of my vision, and I arch into his touch. I can't remember what it's like to feel this. Pain can do that. It can make you forget there are good things in the world and fuck, this is a good thing.

He kisses me again, harder this time. Less cautious. I kiss him back, letting go and giving in. The second I do, pleasure spreads through me, easing everything back and it's like getting hit with a burst of adrenaline.

Gently at first, he pulls his finger back, and slides it home again. He's easing me into it, setting up a rhythm that brushes the tip of his finger inside and the palm of his hand across my clit. That magic —which in my mind shines with sunny light—rises to meet him, sending pulses from where he touches me deep into my core.

Another finger joins the first, and he speeds up, breaking our kiss once more. I open my eyes to his, and we're so close together. His focus is on nothing but me and it's intoxicating.

Suddenly I can feel it coming, the climax that felt impossible. I reach out, holding onto his arm, still holding me close. Pleasure snaps up my spine, and as much as it feels good, it feels like *freedom*. Like I'm shedding weight that was bound to me.

I can feel Brae's magic seeping into me, being used up in the pleasure, making it greater. And I can feel it when it centers, narrowing to just my clit and inside, where he's fucking me furiously with his hand. So fast I can't breathe, I'm gasping and on the edge, ready to go over.

His palm grinds down into my clit, and the wave breaks, carrying me away. It's like stepping into the sun after days in darkness. Magic and pleasure sweep upward through me, banishing any pain. It's fast and sharp, a bright line of sensation drawing a line between me and my agony. Plus it feels fucking fantastic. Ecstasy carrying me away in waves.

I come back to myself in bits. The sensation of breathing hits me first. It's easy, and I don't feel like something is sitting on my chest. Although he isn't moving anymore, Brae is still touching me, and I open my eyes to see him. He's searching my face, and I smile. "It worked," I say. "Thank you."

His face eases into a small smile too. "It was very much my pleasure."

My breath catches, because I can think clearly now. I asked him to help me, and that could have meant anything. He could have just made me come. It didn't have to be intimate or special to get the job done, but it felt that way.

He didn't have to kiss me...

I glance down, and there's no mistaking his arousal through the human trousers that he's still wearing from when he rescued me. His fingers move just slightly on the back of my neck, and I shiver. When I look back up into his eyes, I can see the change.

I'm honestly not sure what it is yet, but something is different. For both of us.

It should have been nothing. So why does it feel like everything?

Brae glances down at my lips, and I think that he might kiss me again. I wouldn't mind. I want to know what his kisses feel like now that I can breathe and feel without the fog of pain. He moves closer, and I hold my breath.

Our lips are a breath apart when I hear the clattering of stone, and I hear Kent's voice explode through the cavern. "What the fuck?"

Brae turns, revealing the others standing in the mouth of the cave. They've brought back something they hunted, and every expression is different. But I can only see Kent and his horror. For the briefest of seconds, I see what he must see: My torn dress shoved up around my hips, with Brae leaning over me, his hand still between my legs.

Verys and Aeric barely catch Kent before he lunges.

CHAPTER TEN

VERYS

I throw my arms around Kent's shoulders as soon as I feel him tense to spring. Aeric does the same. It's not even a conscious movement, just sheer instinct from years of training and observation.

He strains against us, the sound of his struggle echoing off the crystal walls. Kari is saying his name, and I'm distracted for a second because she's on her feet. Standing on her own.

The distraction costs me, and he shoves his elbow into my stomach. This human is strong—stronger than some fae, and even with the two of us holding him back, it's not an easy fight.

Brae is on his feet now, and he's speaking too. They're both trying to explain, but he's not listening, practically screaming with strain. Thank the goddess that he doesn't have fae senses and can't smell the scent of sex that's dripping through this cave.

It's not just the scent of union though, it's *her*. She smells sweet, and that scent sinks down through me, tugging on my gut. I look at her now, and she's upset watching Kent. Instinct takes over, and I rip Kent away from Aeric and slam him down onto the cave floor harder than strictly necessary. "You need to listen," I hiss in his ear. "She's trying to talk to you."

Kent goes still, and I look over at Kari. But now she's speechless, staring at Kent on the ground. Fine. I can make it clear that he's made a mistake. "Violating someone's will is the most serious offense a fae can perform in our court. The sentence is often death, and even if it is not, most do not survive the torment. And, regardless of the punishment, that is not something any one of us would do." He flexes against my hold, and I push him down again. "We've been fighting to keep Kari alive. You keep forgetting that."

Kent twists towards Kari. "You asked for this? Tell me you didn't so I can kill him."

I watch as Kari rises to a height that seems greater than her own, and her face darkens with anger. "Yes, Kent, I asked for it. If you have to know — not that it's any of your business — I tried on my own but was in too much pain. And now there is no pain. I feel *good* for the first time since this happened, and that is entirely thanks to Brae. Are you really so selfish that you wouldn't want that? I do not belong to you."

He goes limp in my hands, and I release him. If there's one thing I've seen, it's that he listens to Kari. When she can get through.

I move away from Kent towards the fire. I don't want to be near him and the look he gives me when he stands. He goes to stand in front of Kari. Brave man. Reaching out, he strokes down both her arms with his hands. I ignore the rolling of my stomach as he does so.

"I just thought..." Kent says, swallowing. "The two of us."

Kari softens and pulls him to her. "I know, and yes. But please stop attacking them. I would be dead if they weren't here."

Kent pulls her into an embrace, and I catch the jealousy in Brae's eyes. I can feel it too, deep in my gut. And I don't understand it. I'm not used to jealousy or...longing.

It's been a long time since I've joined the Carnal Court, and it was never my choice. And in all that time, I've never been tempted like this.

I made my choice a long time ago, and I've never broken it. I'm celibate. I never wanted any part of the Carnal Court magic when my Lunar magic was taken from me. I don't need much to survive. But Kari...something about her is pulling me closer in a way I've never felt before. I know Brae and Aeric are feeling it too. It's a bond that shouldn't exist and that none of us can explain.

Something that all three of us are afraid to put a name to. Once we do, it's real, and we won't be able to turn back.

I move away from her and Brae, as far as I can across the cavern. The scent of her is strong, sweeter than roses but still light. And the fact that Brae touched her, pleasured her, unsettles me in a way that I don't like. There's a prayer for answers to the Goddess on my lips, but I hold it back.

I don't know if I'm ready for the answer.

Regardless of it all, watching Kari stand and stretch, come and sit by the fire without any trace of pain in her movement, that's amazing. She's graceful and fluid. I can't seem to keep my eyes away. Which is why I'm all the way over here. I don't know what to do with this.

"We still have a long way to go," Aeric says. "Can we portal now?"

Brae shakes his head. "I wouldn't risk it. This

curse isn't something I've dealt with, and just because we've tricked it into receding doesn't mean it won't react badly to other forms of magic."

I clear my throat. "We're not far from the Crystal Court. We can ask them for help, more reliable mounts than fae beasts."

"Good idea," Aeric nods. "We're too exposed out here."

"And clothes," Kent adds. "Kari can't keep wearing a dress that's falling to pieces."

No, she can't, though I don't think any of us mind the view.

Kent turns and glares at me, and I realize that I've spoken those words out loud. Shit. Brae has a tiny smirk on his face, Aeric is looking at me like I'm an idiot, and Kari...Kari is looking at me, even though she's blushing.

I can't read the expression on her face, but it isn't angry.

If anything, that look kindles hope inside me. It's more than I've ever had before.

CHAPTER ELEVEN

KARI

I don't know if it's the fact that I feel normal for the first time in what feels like forever, or the leftover feelings from an amazing orgasm, but I'm very aware of all the men in this cave with me—both human and fae. And how utterly gorgeous every one of them is. But I hadn't thought...

Verys's comment came out of nowhere. It was soft and matter-of-fact. He hadn't even realized he said it until a few seconds later. Until a short while ago I hadn't even been capable of thinking about the fact that my dress is ripped and dirty, exposing patches of skin, along with its already scandalous back.

What does he see when he looks at me? That moment between Brae and me made me realize that he could be attracted to me. And I know that Kent is. But Verys has been quiet and steady so far. With his pale skin and silvery hair, he's been very much the angel standing watch. The way he looked at me just now, with a strange longing, makes something stir in me.

I want to know what he's thinking.

It doesn't seem possible that these gorgeous, powerful fae males could want me like that. Why would they? I've been nothing but a burden, barely able to stand. But that doesn't change the fact that Brae said yes and the silver eyes locked with mine are drawing me in, making me wonder what it would have been like if it had been Verys's hand between my legs. Kissing me.

And Aeric is there in my mind too, taking his place. I shift the way I'm sitting, suddenly and fully aroused again, imagining what it would be like to have any of them there. Glancing up at Aeric, he's staring at me hard, and I stifle a gasp.

There's hunger in his gaze. Dark and unbridled lust that sends a blast of heat down my spine. I have to look away, otherwise I'm going to stand and go to him.

God, this can't be happening, can it? It's not possible that these men want me. I can't make sense of it. I shake my head to clear it, ignoring the impulses of my body to reach out to touch them. All of them. Any of them.

"I'm going to get some sleep, now that I can," I say. And as soon as I say it, exhaustion takes over my body. I lay down, my skin still singing, even with the tiny scratches of the cave floor. It's a little strange to be aroused when you're running for your life. But the last few days have been nothing but strange. I should get used to it.

I wake to the sound of popping. Or what I think is popping. The cave is darker than when I went to sleep—like the light is dimming. Maybe it's sunset. Is there a sunset in Allwyn?

Blinking my eyes, I sit up and turn towards the mouth of the cave. It's not popping, it's the sound of feet on stone. Fae beast feet. In front of me are four fae beasts, and like the ones from the jungle, they're beautiful. Horse-like shapes made from crystalline stone and glass.

One looks like it could be lapis and sunstone, another maybe jade. The colors and textures fade from one to another seamlessly. Even though it seems like we're in the worst circumstances, I love it here. Who could have imagined this?

The fae males are standing outside the cave, discussing something, but Kent is standing by one of the creatures and sees me watching. He doesn't say anything, but his eyes are lit with a smile and he gestures for me to come closer.

As I stand, I can feel a twinge. And it's not from sleeping. It's just barely there, but the curse is coming back already. I have some time, but that was fast. When Brae said it would move quickly, I hoped it would last at least a day. Though I don't know how long I've been sleeping.

I reach out and place my hand on the creature's rocky side. It's somehow both hard and soft, and most strangely *alive*. I've never felt a rock that was alive and breathing before. It turns its head and I see a blink, a rust-colored iris with a starry pupil. It expands and contracts, almost like a flower.

"Hi," I say softly. "Thank you for carrying us."

There's a vibration under my fingers, a kind of purr. It's soothing, calming. This creature is good, even if it's called a beast. I can feel it. I close my eyes and rest my forehead against the creature's side, listening to the sound before I sense a presence at my side. Kent.

"How long was I asleep?"

"A few hours. Verys says it's not far to the

Crystal Court, so we're going to try to make it before full dark."

"Okay."

Verys's voice comes from behind me. "And unfortunately you can't ride together. Fae will be wary enough of two humans this deep in Allwyn. It's safer for the two of you to ride separately."

I watch Kent's jaw tense, but he nods before reaching for my hand and squeezing. "Can we have a second?" He waits until Verys slips away again before he sighs. "I'm sorry, Kari. I've been a real ass."

"Yes, you have. I can understand where it came from, but it's not okay."

He swallows. "I know. I wanted to tell you that I get it, and I'm going to get it under control."

There's a little tension that eases in my chest. Pure and sweet relief. I've been a little in love with him for so long, that it was hurting me to see him like this. No matter if his anger was on my behalf or not, it was misplaced. I'm not his to claim. Not yet anyway. "Thank you." I hesitate, fighting the emotion climbing through my chest. "Things would have been so different if I had just let you take me to a party."

Kent pulls me close, and I bury my face in his chest, not wanting him to see just how deeply I wish it could have been. "Maybe," he says softly. "Or maybe she would have found you anyway, and they wouldn't have been close enough to help." His fingers dig into my spine, like he's holding me back from that fate. "You could have died that night. And you're still here. I don't care about any of it, as long as you're alive and safe." He sounds emotional too, but clears his throat. "Can I kiss you?"

I don't say anything, just lift my face to his and let him. It's soft and sure, sweet and yet deep enough to stir need to life inside me. It's what our first kiss should have been.

He pulls back, smiling. "Hi."

"Hello," I say, biting my lip.

There's a footstep behind me, and Verys is there. I nod, and follow him, letting Kent hold my hand until we have to let go.

We approach another of the creatures, this one green and white stone. Its body glistens in the fading light. It purrs too when I approach, and I smile. It's a small thing, but I'm glad that they like me. Here in Allwyn, I'm totally out of place, but if these creatures like me that's something.

Verys helps me up and swings himself up behind me, and we're off. We can travel much faster than the last time we were on fae beasts because I can move faster. I can feel the pain jostling in my bones, threatening to surface, but it's fine, for now.

I was going to ask Verys some questions, about him, and about what he said earlier, but as soon as we start to move, I'm exhausted again, and I let myself drift as we ride. But even then, I can't ignore the way his hand casually rests on my hip, keeping me upright. And the feeling of his body behind mine, warm and solid. I try to push away the thoughts of what it might be like to turn around and kiss him, but I can't.

The stone environment around us shifts, where crystals were mixed with formations of stone, now crystal is the dominant element. Shapes of every size and color explode from the ground, twisting up and around to form tunnels and bridges that we wind through. It reminds me a of some of the cathedrals back in New York, when you'd go in and the sun would shine through the stained glass, coloring everything.

That's what this is like…living inside a kaleidoscope.

"Is everything in Allwyn this beautiful?" I ask quietly. I know he'll hear me.

I feel him shake his head no. "I wish it were. But there are dark places in Allwyn just as there are in the human realm. Darker, even, because things here are amplified."

"What kind of places?" Everyone in the human world has heard the good and bad stories about Allwyn. The immense beauty and wealth and power. But also the people who are lost and never return. The dark horrors that you tell children to hope that they'll never encounter Fae and agree to go with them.

But no one really knows the truth.

"There are courts for everything," Verys says slowly. "Including darkness, pain, and worse things than I care to talk about. Everything has a balance, and so in order to have all this, we must have those things too. But those courts are far away, and if you're lucky, you will never be near them."

"They're really that bad?" I can imagine, but still, it's hard to think about something that dark when I'm bathed in azure light shining through a wave of crystal.

Verys's breath on my skin makes me shiver as he lowers his voice. "Humans may not walk free in those courts. They would break your mind and then your body. You would be lucky if that's all they did, and you would not survive."

I turn my face to look at him. There's nothing in

his face to tell me that he's joking. He's telling the truth. "Oh."

"Don't worry," he says, "The Crystal Court is not one of those places."

"They'll like us?"

He laughs, "I'm not sure, but we are allies."

"I didn't think there were things like that in Allwyn."

We round a spire of crystal that's clear and polished like glass. I can see through it, and we're approaching the court. It's like nothing I've ever seen.

"Fae politics are very delicate and very complex. Because we have thousands of years of relationships that have succeeded and broken, and many wars that have destroyed our trust in each other."

But I'm barely listening to him, because my jaw is on the ground. Shining walls of stone that slip from rose to amethyst to emerald and back again rise before us. They disappear into the distance, and even this far away I feel like I have to tilt my head back to look at them.

Above the wall, spires of white pierce the violet sky, glimmering in the dying light. But none of this is unnatural. My gut tells me none of it has been shaped or carved by fae hands. It's simply been *formed*. Either with the help of magic or by Allwyn itself.

Fae walk the walls, and we're greeted with the sound of tinkling glass, still thin and soft because we're far away. Verys and the other fae lift their hands in greeting. But I don't. I can't seem to take my eyes off the walls and the spires.

As we grow closer, more details come into focus. The walls are translucent, letting some light in and out, and as the sky fades from dark violet to an inky black, the city begins to glow. Light itself moves through the structures, forming patterns that curl outward and fall back on themselves and reform, never stopping.

"Wards," Verys says to me softly.

I nod. Magic. To keep things out. But... "Who do you need to keep out?"

Verys sighs. "It hasn't been so long since the last fae war, and old habits die hard."

I'm curious about that, but we're drawing closer, and I have to lean my head all the way back to see the top of the walls. The movement lands my head on Verys's shoulder, and his hand tightens around my hips. I never asked Verys about his statement, and how he feels. But now that we're entering the court, it doesn't seem like the right time. But I will. I have to know.

The gates to the court are black crystal shot through with red. These are carved with images of fae in battle, in love, and other scenes. The starkness of the black compared to the riot of color around me feels sinister. The two fae with drawn swords awaiting our approach only adds to that sensation.

Brae reaches the gate first, and he makes some kind of hand signal to the guards. They talk, but it's low enough that I can't hear it. The guardians of the gate look at me, the state of my clothes, and they look at Kent as well. Brae talks some more, and they nod.

Aeric dismounts, and Verys helps me down. The beast purrs when I touch it, it's eye seeking mine. "Goodbye, friend."

It vanishes so quickly it seems like it was never there. The others are gone too, leaving us alone with the guards in front of the gates of black stone.

CHAPTER TWELVE

KARI

The gates open with a sound like thunder—cracking stone. Light washes out from the city before us, vibrant and sparkling as it's revealed. I can't take it all in, there's too much, and I'm glad that Verys's hand is on the small of my back, guiding me forward.

I'm escorted into a riot of color and light, and that's just the buildings. They're formed from that same magically-shaped stone, in every color imaginable with light shining from within. The fae around us are just as colorful, with skin and hair in vibrant shades, as well as ones that humans would consider normal. Crystals cover clothing and skin, and everything seems to shimmer. I feel very drab by comparison, still only in my torn dress and covered in the grime of travel.

The air smells sweet, like flowers and spun sugar. I can't tell where it's coming from or if it's just the way the air smells here. The last of the light is fading from the sky, drawing it down into a deeply purple velvet pricked with stars. But they're not the stars I know. These are spread across the sky like glitter frozen mid-air—thousands and sparkling.

It seems like the nightlife of the Crystal Court is starting up, fae wandering the streets in twos and threes, all clearly heading somewhere. It strikes me as familiar and also, so brutally alien.

Verys's hand is still on my back as we're guided onto a street that's also a market, stalls glittering with gems and fabric and potions and charms. Some of the potions look so similar to what I would sell that it makes my chest ache.

"The look on your face is confusing," he says.

"I miss my shop," I say. "But I was also thinking, I don't know what fae *do*. I've never even thought about it, really. Like do you go to restaurants in the evenings or concerts? That seems so...human."

"Enjoying the company of others, or art, is not a strictly human pastime. But yes, many of the things fae do reflect what you would consider to be normal human behavior. Even more so, because we have magic, and don't have to work to live in the same way humans do."

I sigh. "Can't imagine at all why humans are jealous of you."

He laughs, a little freer than I've heard before. Maybe because we're in more familiar territory and safer than we have been. "That's a fair point."

We're in the middle of the street when a fae male with rose-colored skin approaches us, nods to the gate guards that have been escorting us. A cloak darker than his skin flows around him, his hair swept up and around in intricate braids that I don't think I'd ever be able to do. "Welcome travelers. I've been sent to escort you further. You shall have the hospitality of the Crystal Court. Once you have the opportunity to refresh your clothes, our Rialoir would speak with you."

"Of course," Brae says, and we follow him, turning off the main market street onto a smaller one bathed in yellow light from the nearby buildings that look like they might be grown out of citrine.

Kent looks back at me, eyes showing concern, and I smile to tell him that I'm okay. I'm hopelessly lost in the maze of the jeweled buildings, unable to make my eyes stand still. There's so much to see, everything perfect and more beautiful. Even the corners of the buildings have tiny carved details that you could miss if you weren't looking for them. Every color imaginable is here, and it feels like we're walking through a rainbow.

There's a twinge of pain in my stomach, and I suck in a gasp. Nothing I can't handle. For right now, at least. Verys presses closer to me, whispering so softly that only I can hear. "Are you all right?"

"For the moment."

Our guardian stops in front of a building of pale green. It's wider and the base with each level stacked on top smaller, like a little pyramid. "Clothing and refreshments have been prepared for you. I'll escort you to the palace when you've finished."

Verys escorts me inside, and there's a beautiful fae female there, standing with a smile. She has pale skin, almost white, with hair a fiery red that practically glows. "Welcome. I'm to help Kari while the rest of you dress."

Instantly, both Kent and Aeric are in front of me. "There are reasons we seek help," Aeric says, staring her down. "We can't leave her alone."

All she does is raise an eyebrow. "The walls are thin enough to hear her if she calls, and you'll be about ten steps away. After traveling with four men, Kari might like a break from this much... masculinity." Amusement lights her grin. "I promise that no harm will come to her."

It takes him a second, but Aeric relaxes and turns to me. "Will you be all right?"

I nod. I know enough about the fae laws of hospitality that I know her promise not to harm me will be kept. If it is not, she will pay a hell of a price. "I'll be fine."

The fae extends her hand to me, and I take it. She gently pulls me through the curtain filling the doorway to the left, and they're left staring after me.

"My name is Kaya," she says. "I'm very happy you're here."

"Why?"

She grins at me. "I've never met a human before."

"Oh." Her excitement spills over to me, and I can't help but smile back. "I'm a little worse for wear, but I hope I live up to your expectations."

She waves a hand, pausing in front of another door. "I don't have any expectations, but they might."

The space we enter is gorgeous. The pale jade walls of the building fall away and look over a rich garden with a tangle of trees and wildlife that is conspicuously absent from the rest of the Kingdom of Stone. But the lush greenery doesn't seem to be suffering in any way. If anything, it's thriving under the care of these fae who protect it.

In the center of the room is a large, circular pool of water. Steam is rising off it, and the faint eddies rippling across the surface are accompanied by the glow of magic.

Piles of gorgeous fabric are scattered in one corner and in another is a giant mirror at a table with enough make-up that any make-up artist would be absolutely beside themselves. But that's not what Kaya is referring to. Four more fae females are in the room, all stunningly beautiful. They're colored as brightly as this city, one with pink skin as bright as a highlighter, and another who's entirely shades of deep and burnt orange.

Their conversation stops when we enter, and I feel them take me in. My ratty and torn dress, the dirt covering my skin, the exhaustion in my eyes. And they pass judgment.

I've never understood how I could always know how other women felt about me. Maybe it comes from having been in the ballet world for so many years, but I know when the room shifts.

Three of them don't like me. The fourth one isn't sure. But the hostility I instantly see in the other eyes make me hesitate. Maybe Aeric was right, and I should stay with them. This could be some kind of trap.

Kaya promised her hospitality. Are they bound by it too?

"This is the guest?" The female who doesn't seem angry is the one who speaks. Her voice is soft and musical, and I look at her more closely. She has brown skin and hair that matches, though there are streaks of brilliant blue running through it. It reminds me of some bird's feathers, that sudden change in color.

Kaya smiles at me, her hand squeezing my shoulder. "Indeed she is."

"I thought the guests were from the Carnal Court," the orange female says coldly. "She's human."

"There are three members of the Carnal Court, and a human man as well."

A tense silence hangs in the air, and I swallow. Pain blooms in my stomach for a moment, and I hiss through my teeth before it passes. This relief isn't going to last, and dread blooms in my chest. I don't want to go back to that.

Kaya's hand is still on my shoulder. "I have promised Kari my personal hospitality, and she's been extended the hospitality of our Court. If you do not wish to serve our guest, then get out." Her voice leaves no room for argument, and immediately three of them leave, brushing past me with unfriendly force. But the fourth stays, with a small smile on her face.

"I'm sorry," I say when they've exited.

Kaya snorts, which is hilarious coming from someone who looks so ladylike. "Why are you sorry? You did nothing. There are unfortunately still many of our kind who view humans as lesser. As idiotic as that idea is."

The other female steps forward. "And even if you hadn't been human, they were eager to see the fabled males of the Carnal Court. Our courts do not often mix."

A stab of jealousy ignites in my chest, so sharp it takes my breath. "Are they going to serve them?"

"No," Kaya smirks. "Though I am sure they would enjoy that, I do not think your companions would. They seem...very loyal."

"Yeah," I say, that jealous panic still making my heart race. There's no reason for it. No matter what happened earlier, I don't have a claim on any of those men. Even if my body thinks differently.

"I'm Merina," the other female says, taking a step closer. "And you are safe here."

Tears blur my eyes suddenly, and I cover my face in my hands, everything catching up at once. It's so much. Everything is so much. I've been in so much pain that I haven't even had the chance to feel this panic and grief or anything else.

Hands pull mine away from my face. Merina stands there, looking at me kindly. "Everything is going to be all right."

"I'm not so sure," I say.

A piece of cloth flies past me, and I look over to see Kaya digging in the pile. "Of course it is," she chirps. "We are going to help. And those men of yours aren't going to let anything happen to you. Trust me."

Merina smiles and hands me a small cloth to dry my face. "Is there something I should know?"

My tears are still there, but that burst of emotion is fading. I am safe here. Kaya's head pops up from the pile of fabric, her wild red hair exploding around her like a firework. "When I went to fetch Kari, two of them jumped in front of her like I was going to bite."

"I see," Merina says, still grinning.

"I don't see," I say, as she helps me out of the silk I've been wearing for days. Slowly I'm helped into the water, and the heat of it sinks into my bones. "Oh my god," I say. "I had forgotten about hot water."

"How long have you been traveling?" Merina asks.

"I don't know." It's the honest answer. "I've been...unconscious for part of it."

The water feels so good on my skin, like it's pouring energy into me. The little ripples of light that are swimming through it make me suspect that that may actually be the case.

I don't notice that both Kaya and Merina have gone still until I look up. "Did I say something?"

Kaya cocks her head to the side. "Can we ask you what happened?"

I take a breath to speak, and pause. Should I tell them? There's a tiny whisper inside that says I should trust no one. But Kaya gave her promise. She cannot harm me so long as I am here. And she is right. If any of the men suspected I was in danger, I doubt that I would be alone.

"I was attacked," I say softly. "By a fae."

The two of them stare at me with supernatural stillness. I go on. "A fae female. I own a magic shop in the human world. I don't have much magic, just enough to make some charms and potions. She was a customer—or so I thought. I was on the way to a party, and she must have followed me. She attacked me with magic. I don't know why, but it's still inside me." I press a hand to my gut, where I can sense the core of that darkness. "It's killing me."

Merina looks at me like she's trying to figure out

a puzzle. "And how did you come across three fae males?"

"They came across me," I say, scrubbing the dirt from my skin. "They sensed the magic and saved my life."

I'd forgotten what it's like to feel clean. Something so simple that you take for granted.

"And the human man is your lover?" Kaya asks, handing me a glass bottle filled with deep red liquid.

That color matches the blush on my cheeks. "Yes," I say. "No. Not really. We wanted to—before everything happened…It's complicated."

Kaya puts her hands on my shoulders and turns me around in the water, pouring some other substance on my hair and proceeding to wash it. "You don't have to—"

She shushes me, continuing to wash it. I can't remember the last time that someone played with my hair, and it feels nice. Even though these aren't Carnal Fae, clearly they're not shy. And they don't have the same kind of boundaries that humans do when it comes to touch. I'm going to have to remember that.

"So where are they taking you?"

I pour some of the red soap into my hand, distracted by how much it looks like liquid rubies in my palm. Even their bath products look like jewels.

"Their Court. There's a healer there they think might be able to break the curse that's killing me." Kaya pours water over my hair and rinses it out. "It's only been today that I haven't been in pain, but it will come back soon."

Using the soap, I rid myself of the last of the dirt that's build up on my skin and under my nails. I dunk under the water and rinse out the last of the shampoo. God, I could stay in this bath forever. I feel shiny and brand new.

When I surface, the corner of Merina's mouth tips up into a smile. "How did you get rid of the pain?"

My whole body flushes so quickly that it almost burns, and they both burst into laughter. Kaya is grinning and looks at her friend. "I told you." Then she looks at me. "You're a lucky girl."

"Why?"

"To have three males of the Carnal Court as your lovers? Even the most loyal fae could be tempted with an offer like that."

"It's not like that," I say quickly, even though I can't say that I wouldn't want it to be like that. "They're just trying to keep me alive. The curse absorbs a lot of magic."

Kaya reaches for my hand and helps me out of the bath so that I don't slip, and Merina wraps a large, warm towel around me. "I have no doubt that that is true," Kaya says. "But what I saw between you was more than obligation."

I blush again. It can't be true. No matter what I've seen or heard, the hunger in Aeric's eyes and Verys's words, Brae's pleasure. I'm just a human. Four men can't want me. Especially three fae gods of pleasure. "It's impossible."

"It's not," Merina says lightly. "And you should know that things here are not like the human world." She pulls me around the pool and sits me down at the table with all the make-up.

"What do you mean?"

Merina perches herself on the edge of the table. She shrugs. "There are less female Fae than male Fae. Sharing a partner is more normal here."

She says it so simply. *Sharing a partner.* As if it's that easy, just to decide that you can be with more than one person. There's a little piece of me that asks why it shouldn't be that easy? But even if it's common here, it's not real. It's not like that. They don't feel that about me.

Kaya makes a frustrated noise. "I swore the last time that I was here there was a beautiful green fabric."

"The one that Amaya took for herself?"

"No," she says absently, "though that was

beautiful as well. This one is much richer, and it'll be perfect with her coloring."

I realize that she's going to *make* me clothes. "Oh, you don't have to make me anything," I say. "I can have whatever is lying around. I'm sure it's going to get dirty as soon as we leave."

Merina starts to laugh as she's looking through different pots of color on the table. "That's a fight you will not win. Kaya is one of the best designers in the Crystal Court, and she's always wanted to make something for a human to wear. And trust me," she whispers, "whatever she creates for you will be stunning."

"It *will!*" Kaya says, flying out of the mountain of fabric victoriously. She has a shimmering emerald fabric in her hands, and I'm stunned by its beauty. So much that I barely hear the rest of what she's saying. "But I'm not going to just make you a dress. Especially after the way your last one ended up—which looked like it was amazing when it wasn't battle-scarred—I'll make you some travel clothes too. Which will of course be fabulous as well as functional."

A laugh flies out of my lips so fast that I pause. It's been forever since I've *really* laughed. Or at least it's felt that way. It feels good, like my soul is a little lighter.

I can feel that pain in my gut. It's growing, but for this brief moment it doesn't matter. "Why are you making me a dress?"

"Because you're going to meet the Rialoir and Rialoia—the King and Queen," Merina says. "You've asked for aid, and the Rialoir must hear what's happened to you. Especially if whoever is chasing you has followed you into our Kingdom."

"Okay."

"Hold still," she says, starting to paint my face with something pale.

"I didn't realize that fae used make-up. Can't you just use magic to look how you want?"

"We could," Merina says. "And sometimes we do if it's something big. But glamours are both difficult to do and more difficult to hold for a long time. It ends up being *much* more fun to create make-up in the colors you want that won't fade no matter how many times you decide to fall into the mead fountain on Beltane."

There's definitely a story there, and Merina winks at me when I raise my eyebrow in question. "That makes sense."

"Stand up for a second," Kaya says, "and drop the towel."

I hesitate, and she rolls her eyes. "Humans and your modesty. I already saw you naked in the bath."

She has a point, and I place the towel on the chair I was sitting on while she stares at me clinically. I whisper to Merina. "What is she doing?"

"She's memorizing your measurements and figuring out what looks good on you so she can make your clothes."

"All done!" Picking up the fabric, which shimmers and shines, both dazzling and subtle. "I'm going to make you a dress that proves me right."

I blink. "What are you proving?"

"That those delightfully handsome men that are protecting you have far more on their mind than just your safety."

I blush, and my stomach flips, but I don't say anything. I just turn back to Merina, who has the same conspiratorial smile on her face, and let her continue to paint my face.

CHAPTER THIRTEEN

AERIC

Through the walls I can hear the muffled sounds of the females and Kari speaking. Even better, I can hear her *laughing*. It's a sound that I've never heard before, and everything in me reacts to it. That tide pulling me toward her is lit up with that sound, and for a second, I allow myself to believe that this is true and that everything will be fine.

But only for a second. We're still being hunted, and as much as the thought feels like a sword is being punched into my gut, the chance that Kari could die before we reach Urien is high.

Please.

I release that prayer to the Goddess. It's been on my lips and in my mind, and I don't pretend that I know what I'm asking for. If it's for her survival, or for this bond we share to be a dream, or for her to want it too. There's too much, and all I can find in myself to ask is *please*.

Kari's laughter slips through the wall again, and I see Brae smiling across the room. I'm not the only one who feels lighter hearing it. It reminds me of all the things that we don't know about her and have yet to discover. We feel so connected because we're running, and we've been trying to save her, but I don't even know her favorite color.

Brae now knows what it feels like to kiss her, and the way her face looks like when she's lost in pleasure. Lucky bastard.

"They'll give her her own room," Verys says.

I look up from the water where I'm sitting. The pool we're sharing is huge and steeped in natural magic that is slowly sinking into my skin. Even if we hadn't been running from a sadistic bitch-fae this bath would make me feel on top of the world. "What?"

Verys looks towards the wall that's separating us from Kari. "We're safe here, as far as alliances go. We're not going to be attacked from within the Court. But this female isn't exactly afraid. She's brazen. She attacked Kari on the street."

Brae nods. "We'll watch her room then."

Kent is looking back and forth between us from

the corner of the pool. He hasn't said much to any of us, which is not exactly surprising. But he hasn't bitten our heads off either, which some would consider progress. "I'll take a watch too," he says.

I look at him, and he meets my eyes. There's determination there, not the possessiveness that I expected. "All right." Kent is a capable human, and on more than one occasion he's shown his strength. I know that he'll fight to protect Kari with all of his will, and he'll be able to rouse us quickly enough to make a difference.

"Are we going to tell them everything?" Kent asks.

I'd been thinking about it, weighing both the pros and the cons. "I think we should. There's very little risk in doing so, and if we're followed here after we leave, they can be aware and possibly pass us more information."

He nods, accepting that verdict without any struggle. I know that he and Kari spoke before we left the cave. Whatever she said to him must have had an impact. I can't say I that don't sympathize with him. Were I in his position, I would struggle similarly. It's definitely for the best that he doesn't know about the way we're connected to Kari. He might be doing better, but there's only so much someone can take.

The door opens, and we all go to attention. It's simply a male fae with some clothes that he leaves for us. Brae speaks, mostly to Kent. "We've been extended the hospitality of the Rialoir. Not only does that mean that no one of the Crystal Court can harm us while we're here, but he'll provide everything that we need to continue on our journey."

"Why would he do that?" Kent's voice sounds genuinely curious.

Verys stretches and exits the water. "The Carnal and Crystal court have been close allies for a very long time. It's one of the most stable relationships we have with an external court. If someone sought help in the Carnal Court, our Rialoia would extend the same courtesy."

It's true, though people who visit the Carnal Court aren't often looking for supplies and protection. They're looking for pleasure, which we're more than happy to provide.

I'm loath to leave this bath, because the water is replenishing my magic, and it feels excellent to be clean and whole. But we must. Hospitality or not, the Rialoir is expecting us, and we should not keep him waiting the whole night.

The clothes that have been left for us are of the highest quality—of course—and they fit perfectly.

We've all been given a similar style, colors varying between us. The clothes I've been given are black, the fabric of the shirt and vest shimmering with crimson in the light. I like it.

Then I see the back of the vest, and I grin. This should be entertaining. The vest has laces in the back, and the body is structured, with boning in the material. To Kent's eyes, when he sees it, it will appear much like a human corset, though the style of clothing was worn by Fae far longer than it was worn by humans. And it's a male custom here, which I'm sure will be strange to him.

Dressing quickly, I send a sliver of magic up my back, tightening the laces and tying them off. Brae and Verys do the same and begin buckling their weapons back on. It is not customary to appear armed before royalty, but in this circumstance, it's necessary.

Kent picks up his vest, which is a rich turquoise, and there's plenty of confusion that he doesn't want to show us. He turns away, trying to figure it out, but it doesn't work well and his first attempt has him tangled in the laces. The second attempt goes better, though the vest is hanging off loosely, as he cannot reach the laces.

I shoot a conspiratorial glance at Brae, who's already smiling, and I send a burst of magic towards

Kent. He jumps as the laces cinch tight at his back, forcing him to stand tall. Whirling on us, there's fire in his eyes. But all three of our expressions are blank and uninterested. What he doesn't know about who laced him into the corset, the better.

"How do you breathe in these?" He asks.

Verys covers a smile with his hand. "Your body will adjust, and it will loosen as the night goes on."

Kent mutters something under his breath. I didn't catch it all, but I'm pretty sure it had something to do with us being bastards.

More laughter flutters through the wall, and my chest tightens. I want to hear that sound again without a wall between us. "Do you think she's ready?" I ask.

"Only one way to find out," Brae says.

CHAPTER FOURTEEN

KARI

"I think you're just about perfect," Kaya says, adjusting a fold in the skirt of the dress she's wrapped me in. It's formed of that shimmering fabric, shot through with another cloth that is so black it could be made of void itself, and I think it might be the most beautiful thing that I've ever seen.

The skirt falls from my hips in flowing waves that at once look like leaves and water, the bodice twists around my body and up, leaving one shoulder bare, and finishes by twisting down one arm and wrapping around my middle finger.

Merina's work can't be ignored either, because the make-up she's done is stunning. My eyes are smoky and sexy, and my lips shine with a gloss that smells like fresh lilacs and is so light that it feels like nothing. My hair is loose, pinned back so that it tumbles down behind my shoulders in softly curling waves. I'm left standing in front of the mirror, gaping at their handiwork.

Both of them are grinning, waiting for me to say something. Anything. "I—" I clear my throat. "There aren't words."

"I knew this color would be perfect," Kaya says. "Didn't I say?"

Merina is laughing now. "You did."

"*And*," Kaya steps up next to me and takes my hand, sliding it inside a fold in the fabric. "Look."

"You gave me pockets?" My chest lights up with pleasure, and I slip both my hands into them. "Why?"

"I hear things," she says. "And one of the things that I heard is that women in the human world are never given pockets. Is this true?"

I nod, but I'm laughing. "Yes, for the most part it's true."

"Well," Merina says, picking up a small box from the table of make-up. "Since you have the pockets, you need something to put in them."

She hands the box to me, and it's tiny. It's made of a blue, iridescent material that looks like it could be pearl or even opal. There's a small silver clasp on the front, and I pop it open. Inside is what looks like finely ground potpourri, or maybe a mixture of cooking spices. The scent drifting up from the box is amazing, apple and vanilla and a hint of oak. "What is it?"

The two females share a knowing glance, and the light shines off of Merina's raven and turquoise hair. "It's medicine," Merina says. "To prevent pregnancy. One pinch is all you need after a night."

I snap the box shut. Suddenly I'm so hot that I'm sweating. "You don't understand," I say. "I'm not sleeping with them."

"But they are giving you pleasure, are they not?" Kaya asks.

"Yes, but—"

"In our experience," Merina cuts me off, "pleasure leads to more pleasure. Take it, even if you don't think you'll need it."

I have to keep my eyes on the floor, because this is so strange. In the heat of the moment with Brae, everything seemed so natural, and my arousal after was connected to all four of those men. Even so, I'm not used to talking about the possibility of fucking multiple men like it's normal. There were plenty of people in the company that slept around and talked about it. Odette and Emma were never shy about their sex lives.

But I was.

Maybe because I honestly didn't have a regular enough sex life to speak of. Boyfriends were few and far between, and those I was with were normal. It wasn't like this.

A fresh blush stains my cheeks, and I snap the lid of the box closed and tuck it into my pocket.

"You're embarrassed?" Kaya is looking at me in distress.

"Yes," I say. "No. I'm not sure."

Merina reaches out and takes my hand. "There is nothing to be embarrassed about. You are in Allwyn. No one will shame you for taking your pleasure or asking for what you need. You do not need that kind of shame here."

"Thank you."

Kaya frowns. "It seems the human world could stand to learn a few things."

"More than a few," I say.

"Well then," she says, perfect confidence infusing her form again, "I shall just have to travel to the human world and make sure they understand."

"I would love to see that," I say, laughing. "You would take New York by storm. I know some humans who would kill to be dressed by a fae, even if that fae chose to dress them in nothing but leaves and thread. You could be queen of the fashion world."

For a moment, she pauses. "I shall think about that. Right now, your companions are waiting for you, and so is the Rialoir."

Merina waves. "We shall see each other again!"

Kaya loops her arm through mine and walks me back through the maze of hallways. "I very much would like to see you again," Kaya says. "After you are healed. You can tell me more about becoming a queen of New York."

"I'd like that," I say, just before she's swept me up in a hug that's both bone-crushing and tender at once.

"Enjoy tonight," she whispers. "However that enjoyment presents itself to you."

And then she's gone, and I'm alone just inside the front door. I can hear voices on the other side of the door. *Their* voices. Kent, Brae, Aeric, and Verys. It's a soft murmur of masculine sound, and suddenly I'm nervous. They're going to see me in this dress and this make-up and…what are they going to think? The little box in my pocket seems suddenly heavy.

Nausea rolls up through me from my stomach, pain slicing out into my limbs in a flash before it dissipates. I can still breathe. I'm still fine. I can do this. Before I open the door, I make sure that my expression is neutral and there's no sign of the pain that I just felt. If I express any pain at all, they will know.

I open the door and step out into the portico. The men are standing at the base of the steps, and when I step out, Verys and Brae go silent. They're already facing me. Kent and Aeric are not, and it takes them a beat to hear their companion's silence and turn.

All their eyes are burning into me, each expression different, and yet there's one thing that's the same: heat. That heat floods my body in a flush.

Verys seems stunned, standing utterly still and staring. Brae's expression contains an awe that I don't understand and that I do not feel I deserve. In Aeric's eyes I see that same hunger that I saw earlier today—the kind that knocks my breath away and makes me wonder what he's thinking, and what he would do if we were alone.

I see that same desire in Kent's face along with something deeper. More sure. But all of their gazes are on me as I descend the steps to them. None of them have said a word, and I can't help but think that Kaya is *very* good at what she does. The dress certainly makes an impact.

A good one, I think.

"Hi," I say softly.

Brae is suddenly in front of me, capturing my hand and pulling it to his lips. "You look lovely."

"Thank you."

I take in their appearances then, and holy shit, I haven't seen any of them look like this before. Granted, we've been on the run without rest, but even if we hadn't, this would be a good look. Smooth fabrics and rich colors formed into trousers and shirts, over which they each wear a layered vest. The one that Brae has on looks like there might be boning in it. Each one of them is tailored to the person, and it makes every bit of difference.

Their clothes show off the power in their bodies without sacrificing the style or grace. Even Kent, who seems a bit uncomfortable in the foreign clothing, looks *damn* good.

I'm staring at them and they're staring at me, and yet none of us know what to say. Before anyone can, the rose-skinned fae male appears again, and Verys offers me his arm. I take it, letting him guide me away. But this time his hand on my skin feels different. It's probably everything that Kaya and Merina said. I have to be imagining it.

Right?

Maybe.

Those stares didn't feel like nothing.

But immediately my mind tells me that it can't be real. That it's impossible. That it's not right or proper. I never thought that I really cared about what was right and proper, but I never considered this possibility either. If that's what's happening. Oh god, how do I even untangle this?

Aeric is walking next to our escort, and though they're speaking softly, I see that he's looking around, making sure that we're safe and that he's totally aware of our surroundings. Ever the protector.

Verys's voice is quiet enough that only I can hear him speak. "Are you all right? Were they kind to you?"

"I'm fine," I swallow. "And they were lovely. The ones that stayed. Why?"

Glancing over, I see a tiny smile playing on his lips. "I can practically hear your thoughts buzzing. You're anxious." I open my mouth to ask him how he could possibly know that, but he beats me to it. "Your face is easy to read. Your emotions are always near the surface. It's one of the reasons watching you in so much pain is difficult for us."

"One of the reasons?" I breathe. "There are other reasons?"

Kent appears on my other side before Verys can answer. "Kari, look."

We're approaching the palace at the center of the Crystal Court, and the source of the impossibly tall white spires that we saw outside of the city. Now that we're in front of it, it's like walking into the most beautiful dream. The palace itself is white like the spires, some parts of it clear like glass, and the white occasionally bears streaks of colors so pure an artist could never capture them.

I was so caught up in my own thoughts, that I forgot to look around. There's so much to see, every exquisite detail whether it's the garden of stone and crystal flowers that blooms on the side of the street to shops and stores that hold beautiful trinkets that humans can only dream of.

I'm soaking in everything around me, overwhelmed with the beauty of it all. I want to remember every second, but there's so much that I'll never be able to. Maybe I'll be able to come back, explore and enjoy it when my life isn't at stake.

But I notice that I'm not the only one who's staring. There's a fair amount of fae who watch us pass with open curiosity. If Kaya has never met a human before, I'm guessing that the few humans who manage to travel to Allwyn rarely get this far. Or perhaps they're generally unwelcome. But unlike the females who refused to be in the same room with me, I don't sense hostility in these stares, merely interest in something new, perhaps wondering about the circumstances for our visit and the strange composition of our party.

Outside the gates of the palace, we pass a building that's even more beautiful. The stone of the structure erupts from the ground like it grew that way, rising up into the form a blooming rose that's tipped towards the sky as if seeking light. The pale stone shifts color as I watch, a giant opal flower. Fae enter and exit reverently, and it's not until I see the fae dressed in simple white robes that I realize it's a temple to the Goddess. The fae deity, the source of their magic, and the protector of this incredible world.

I'm drawn to it. There's a need so fierce in my chest that I take a step towards it before being halted by Verys's hand. His face searches mine, and I want to know what he's looking for. Then he nods. "We will seek the guidance of the Goddess before we leave the city," he says.

Yes.

A small voice inside says. Good.

That urgent pull releases me, and we're ushered through the gates of the palace—monumental gates of black and grey stone even more imposing than the ones at the edge of the city.

More fae guardians protect this gate, uniforms

starkly white and black with broadswords and bows strapped to their backs. The variety of colors in the fae is made even more vibrant because of their stark clothing and the icy glow of the palace.

The same effect occurs inside, where every color that's put in front of the pale and clear crystal seems rich and pure in comparison. Even my companions seem more alive. I get caught up in staring at Aeric's green skin and the crimson shimmer of his clothing. Brae's honey coloring is warm and inviting and reminds me of his magic and the moments we share together.

I look down to hide the flush on my cheeks from that thought. He didn't say no. He kissed me like we were lovers. There's the smallest chance that Kaya was right. Even if it seems impossible.

My own dress is nearly glowing against the white floor, and I see intricate carvings beneath our feet. Abstract designs of flowers and animals and stones. Stories too, like I've seen before. This court likes to record their history in stone so that it's never forgotten, and I resist the urge to reach down and feel the relief of the carving.

We're escorted through a long hallway with vaulted ceilings that remind of the cathedrals back in New York, with stained glass windows that I'm sure are not actually glass. They're intricate, with stories and images just as detailed as the other carvings, and I would love to see them during the daylight, back-lit and shining through. This hallway is probably a riot of color then, lending an entirely different atmosphere.

I hear the music before I see it, lively and joyous, and at once beautiful. At the end of the hallway is a tall archway of the same white stone, opening onto a space that's even larger. Through it, I can see swirling colors as fae dance in complicated patterns that I can barely follow.

The whole room is too much to take in. The ceilings vault so high that they recede into dimness, though there are spots of colored light that illuminate fluted, arching, circles. It's like little bits of magic got lost and floated up to the ceiling.

In this room, the white and clear stone that makes up the rest of the palace is nowhere present. This is the very embodiment of the Crystal Court.

The walls are made of jagged crystal formations, colors flowing on into the next. Amethyst, ruby, flame, lapis, emerald, onyx, stones that shimmer and some that shine like stars. The floor beneath my feet is polished so the reflections in it appear perfectly. A warm blue stone cut in half, that for all the world makes me feel like I'm walking on petrified water.

The edges of the crowd of dancers notice us as

we enter, and I can almost feel the ripple of whispers whirl through the room.

I can see the King—or Rialoir, as I was told the title is in Allwyn—through the crowd of dancers, and he's not what I expect. When I think of a King, I see an old man with graying hair and a crown. The fae sitting on the throne is young and hale, dressed entirely in crimson. It looks fierce against skin of deep brown, and on the throne by his side is an equally beautiful female. Her skin is pale blue, hair white, and she's delicate. But her clothes match her husband in blood-red crimson, and I know that though she looks delicate, she is not.

The Rialoir raises a hand, and the music falls into silence, a few stray notes leaving bouncing echoes in the silence. The crowd parts, and we're led up to the two thrones, which are utterly clear and smooth. Their facets cast rainbows around the room, landing on the walls and the fae and on me. I can only imagine the effect of the sun. What is it like to sit on a throne that's made of diamond?

We stop just short of the thrones, and Kent and I follow suit when the fae bow to the pair sitting on them. They're both looking at us with open and fervent curiosity. When he speaks, the Rialoir's voice is resonant and easily fills the entire space. "Welcome to the Crystal Court."

"Thank you, Rialoir."

"This was well worth my hospitality," he says, sharp gaze fixing on me. "I'm eager to hear why such a strange group is traveling on foot through Allwyn. But first, we shall eat."

CHAPTER FIFTEEN

KARI

*I*t's been hours, and still the banquet is going. The Rialoir had waved his hand, and the huge room was filled with tables absolutely laden with food. Some of the most amazing edible creations that I've ever seen, even though my plate is still empty.

All five of us were seated near the Rialoir and Rialoia, and we told the story. Or rather, mostly the fae told the story. The Rialoia kept glancing at me in sympathy as they spoke, but I didn't say anything. For the most part, I had been unconscious, and I wasn't about to tell the rulers of the Crystal Court that I needed to masturbate in order to stay alive. I did fill in the bits in New York before Allwyn.

But when the story reaches its current point, the Rialoir turns to me. "You saw your attacker?"

"Yes."

It is the queen—the Rialoia's—voice this time. "Would you permit me to see her?"

"How?"

"There is a priest at the temple who can access memory. Before you depart, I would like to see this fae." The deadly poison in her voice makes me shiver, and I know that if the female that attacked me ever crosses paths with this queen, she will not survive.

"Of course," I say.

"Thank you."

I see the Rialoir take her hand and pull it to his lips, kissing it softly before leaning over and kissing her. Deeply and proudly, not at all embarrassed or hesitant. She returns his kiss, and when he pulls away, her eyes glistened with pleasure and love. He looked at her in the same way, and the pang of longing in my chest is enough to make me reach up and make sure I don't have an actual wound.

I decide I want that. I want exactly that. Bold and unashamed love. He catches me staring, and smiles. But the smile fades when he looks down and sees the empty plate in front of me. "Kari, you are welcome here, and my guest. Are you not hungry?"

All three fae males around me snap to attention, suddenly noticing that I haven't eaten and wondering why. They all look at me with concern, and I can feel them asking if the pain has returned enough to prevent me from eating. But it's not that, and they hadn't noticed there's no food on Kent's plate either. I open my mouth and close it again.

"Forgive me," I say. "I did not know how to ask."

"Ask?" The Rialoia's voice reaches me.

"There are stories in the human world about the dangers of eating fae food. Very few of those stories about fae have turned out to be true so far, but—"

"But because you already have been attacked once by fae, you did not know for sure if the food would trap you in Allwyn?" She asks, a sympathetic smile on her face.

I squeeze my eyes shut in embarrassment, but I don't immediately hear laughter. When I open them again, the Rialoir is looking at me in confusion. "There are stories of humans being trapped by fae food?" He looks fascinated, and his wife beside him seems amused. "Please, tell me more. And I assure you that nothing you eat will keep you here or harm you in any way."

And so Kent and I share the worst fae stories and rumors humans had created throughout the years, and the fae confirm which portions of the stories are true. Not many. Ash wood is extremely painful to the fae, and no one has ever known why. Some of the stories came out of isolated incidents or were blown out of proportion.

In return, both the rulers and fae around us share stories of the human world that have Kent and I laughing as we eat. And we *eat*.

Bread lighter than air, with jams from exotic fruits and warm honey from flowers only found in fae realm, send me straight into bliss. Every flavor is enhanced. Fae fowl with citrus glaze cut through with sharp spice. Sweet rose cakes filled with sticky white chocolate and frosting that could be seriously addictive. Goblets of peach mead that is both cooling and warming at once. Greens sprinkled with ginger and lemon. Small bowls of sherbet that taste of lavender and cream and cardamom.

It's so much food that I barely remember that I haven't eaten much the last few days. The magic that's been keeping me alive also set aside my need for food, or so Brae told me. But the minute the food touched my lips I wanted more, and I eat till I am full. More than full. And now, hours later filled with dancing and conversation, I'm starting to feel sleepy. The fae of the Court aren't showing any signs of exhaustion, and I'm jealous of their stamina.

"Will you dance with me?" The words are soft and come from behind me. I hadn't even noticed

Brae leave his chair a couple of seats down and approach.

Looking out at the crowd, I see the intricate steps that flow from the dancers as smoothly as butter, and I hesitate. In our conversation about fae misconceptions, we already covered the fact that I won't be compelled to dance to death if I start. But even as a trained dancer there's no way I'll be able to keep up with that. "I don't know the steps."

"You don't have to," he says, smiling softly. "I'll lead."

He holds his hand out to me, and this feels like another one of those moments—a choice to go forward or back. I take his hand, and he pulls me up from my chair in one graceful motion. We approach the other fae, and I watch them as they move. It seems so in unison, like they must have practiced for hours or years.

Brae pulls me against him, and I'm swept up into the music. I understand. The music is the magic. I don't have to think about the steps. They're there in my mind. All I have to do is breathe, and I know what to do. Breathing is a little difficult when I'm pressed up against Brae, the reminder of his body and what he did to me with just a hand.

What could he do with more?

Strings weave their melody and sounds that are

deeper. Not human instruments. Sounds that speak of the earth and stone, and everything that makes up this beautiful Court. I move with it. With him. With them. And I'm not surprised by the stories of the endless dancing. I feel like I could do this forever.

God, how long has it been since I danced? Really danced? At one point in my life I thought it would be impossible to forget the freedom of this feeling, but it's all come rushing back, and the joy that breaks through my chest carries me higher. I can't keep the smile off my face as Brae pulls me closer and we weave through the other couples dancing. In and out, back and around. We join together and break apart and coming back to dancing feels like freedom.

Verys takes Brae's place so effortlessly, I don't even miss a step. I can't help but notice the ways in which he touches me differently. His fingers are careful, like I'm fragile. And yet, when he looks at me, it's not like something broken or soft. It's with a longing that steals my breath and almost makes me stumble. I want to kiss him and see what his eyes will do then and what he'll do with that longing if I give him permission.

Aeric steps into the dance with equal ease, and again the energy of the dance shifts. His hands are possessive, holding me tight against his body so I can feel absolutely all of him. So close that I can't see his face. His lips are at my temple, and they don't move, though I want them to. I want to tilt my face upwards and see the hunger that I know is there. God, what is happening to me? I don't look, because I know that if I do something is going to break open inside me, and I don't know if I'm ready. How can you ever be ready for this?

Aeric hesitates before passing me to Kent, but he does it. And we're not as smooth together, two humans dancing among the fae. The music has caught him too, and he smiles, just as overcome with joy as I am. Soon we're spinning in circles, practically abandoning the dance, the melody carrying our steps together. I fit with Kent. I've always fit with him. Dancing with him feels comfortable and safe, while at once stirring to life those fantasies I've had of him — of us — in the back of my shop.

The music swirls and hit a crescendo before ending, echoing up into the ceiling. I come out of the trance I've been in, catching my breath, and realize that we were the only ones still dancing. How long had it been like that? Was I the only one with all four of them? But the Court is clapping and smiling.

Across the room I see Kaya grinning, and Merina, beside her, winks at me.

It's a habit long ingrained in me, I curtsy in the ballet style. I'm not embarrassed. This is what I love, and I'm glad they enjoyed it, even if I barely remember what the dance was or how it went. I'll probably never know.

Kent smiles at me. "Maybe we could count this as the party I was supposed to take you to."

"I'd like that," I say.

He walks me back to our table, and the pain overwhelms me for a moment. I hadn't felt it the entire evening, like joy and conversation were somehow a barrier to it coming back, but it slithers out from its dormant hiding spot, clinging to my bones and rendering me still for a moment. Gripping the back of my chair is the only thing that keeps me upright.

Verys is next to me a second. "Perhaps we should retire."

The energy that the music poured into me is gone, and exhaustion is creeping in. Too many sleepless nights on the run, too much magic taking its toll on my body. "Yes."

Our guide from earlier appears at the Rialoia's summons, and we follow him to the rooms that have been prepared in the palace. We each have our own, all clustered together. We stop as one at my door, and I have to face them all looking with concern. "Do you need help?" Verys asks softly, and I'm not sure if he's asking about getting dressed or if I need another dose of pleasurable magic, but I'm fine.

"No," I say, looking at each of them. If Kaya were here, she might be yelling at me to invite them inside. And yet I'm not ready for that yet. Not like this. "Thank you for dancing with me," I say. "That's the most fun I've had in a long time."

No one but Kent knows about my ballet history, and none of them know that I'm talking about well before the attack. But they don't have to know that now. I turn towards the door and Kent calls after me. "Goodnight, Kari."

"Goodnight."

I close the door softly behind me, and I hear a few murmured words between the men before the shutting of more doors. It only takes me a few moments to take off the beautiful dress and change into one of the simple silk nightgowns that have been left for me. My energy is slipping away, and I barely make it under the covers before I'm pulled under into deep, bottomless sleep.

CHAPTER SIXTEEN

KARI

Hands tear me open. Pale, female hands with nails like talons. I scream, fighting against the pain, but I can't. It rips through me, shattering whatever I have left to fight with. Crimson light is pulsing under my chest and I can't breathe.

She found me. I don't know how she found me. I'm surrounded by darkness, the only light coming from my chest in a ghastly parody of a lantern. I manage to bring my hands to my chest, and it's whole. There are no gashes, no other hands, no wounds, and yet I can't stop screaming because I *feel* them. My skin is hot. I'm burning.

All I can taste is ash and rotten and death. In and out reminding me that she's here to kill me. That she won't stop until I'm dead.

A booming sound shocks through me, and a low voice cursing. There's weight on top of me, a face lit by crimson and I scramble to get away. "Kari."

That's not her. It's not her voice.

"Kari, look at me."

I can't look. How can I look when I can't see? Can't breathe?

Hands grip the sides of my face. "Kari, breathe. Look at me. *Please*." The desperation snaps my eyes to his. Aeric. It's Aeric. "I need you to say yes."

No, I shake my head. I won't say yes to this pain. Never to this pain. Not while I have any life left. She won't take me.

Aeric's lips are at my ear, the words sinking through me. I can hear. I can understand. "Focus as much as you can, Kari. Listen to me. You need magic. I need to touch you. I need your consent."

Oh. *Oh*. Yes.

New pain erupts from that invisible wound, licking down my spine, binding every bone with ruby fire. The pain is fighting him, trying to take me first. He's still speaking to me, telling me what I need. I can let him if I can find my voice. It's somewhere here still. It has to be. "Yes."

I hear myself, voice hoarse from screaming and weak from pain, but I said the word.

Magic flows into me, a wave of cool and

refreshing power. It's sharp with spices—cinnamon and cardamom and nutmeg. It crushes the taste of rotten and ash, soothing as it flows. Dampening her power. But it's not gone. The magic feels like a cool breeze flowing through trees, and I realize that I'm thinking. I can *think*, the curse deep inside newly drawn to Aeric's magic instead of my body. But not for long. It's already restless.

Aeric's weight is still on me, pinning me to the bed as his magic pours from his soul into mine. "Say yes again," his voice is deeper this time. A command.

"Yes," I breathe.

His lips are on my skin then, pressing a kiss to my collarbone. His face is no longer lit with the light of infernal magic, but rather with his own, hands glowing as he drags them down my body. There's nothing but the thinnest nightgown separating us, and then there's nothing at all as he shoves it up below my breasts. Need rises to meet his touch on my skin, leaving me utterly breathless. His magic follows the path of his lips, settling low in my gut and adding to my arousal.

Aeric pushes my thighs apart. My heart is pounding with anticipation. I want this. I want that fire and hunger that I've seen in his eyes. I want him to show me how it feels.

There's a brush of a kiss on my clit, and my body shudders with desire. It was so light I think I may have imagined it. But it doesn't matter. I need more.

"Say yes," Aeric says. There's no doubt about what he's about to do. Save me. Pleasure me. Devour me.

"Yes." It's more a moan than a word now.

I don't have time to breathe before his mouth is on me, and I want to scream again. This time for an entirely different reason. Aeric is licking me outside and his magic is doing the same from the inside, growing and sparking and cascading through me, already starting to banish that pain as if it never existed. His hands slide under my hips, drawing me closer to his mouth so he can ravage me with lips and teeth and tongue.

My pussy is soaked, and he's lapping me up like I'm the best drink there is, not giving my body a chance to question this pleasure or back away from it. It's perfect, sinful, gorgeous. Magic spins outward, flinging itself into every corner of me. I'm dragged through devastating pleasure, vision going white.

The climax takes me fast. Dizzying ecstasy coiling up and out and twisting through me again and again. I arch off the bed, shaking and spent from power and bliss. I'm bathed in the energy of new magic created by the pleasure Aeric is gifting me with. I can feel it pushing back the curse until it's nothing. Little more than a pinprick in my gut.

Just like with Brae, it feels like becoming someone new when I'm released from the hold of the dark magic. I collapse back onto the bed, panting. Fuck, yes. I should have told them it was coming back. I should have never let it get to this point, where I could barely speak.

I expect Aeric to pull back, but he doesn't.

"Aeric—" his name turns into a moan on my lips as he flicks his tongue across my clit once again. His touch isn't forceful now. It's teasing and light, but just as arousing. He's moving over me, brushing his lips over my thighs. Little bites and licks, surprising me each time in a new place. Lips closed, he kisses that tiny bud of nerves, featherlight. I can feel his breath on my skin, and even that small sensation leaves me aching.

Aeric licks me, tongue slipping inside, and I let out a moan. It feels so good—slick and deeply intimate. He presses further, harder, consuming me, stroking inside, fucking me with his mouth. It's too much all at once and I'll also never have enough.

Reaching down, I weave my fingers into that perfect hair, and Aeric grabs my wrists. In a second he has them pinned at my sides while he licks up my pussy back to my clit. I'm anchored to him, pulled against him, held still while he pleasures me, and I shiver.

There's a new burst of wetness, of arousal, and he laps that up too before sealing his mouth over me, sucking fiercely. Aeric's tongue works my clit in sure, long strokes. Over and over, the motion taking me a little higher with each delicious movement. Cool magic pours into me again, and my eyes fall closed.

I've never felt anything like this. Pleasure that's sharp like a knife, carrying me along the edge of orgasm but never pushing me over. I'm drowning in it, writhing under his mouth. Everything I do now is to try to get that little extra bit of pleasure. I beg him for it, force my hips closer to his tongue, try to pry my wrists out of his grasp so I can do it myself, and nothing works. He just continues that slow, steady teasing of my clit until I relax, surrendering to it and to him.

My orgasm rolls in like a tide this time. Slow, sure, and steady. My breath comes in gasps, and my whole body going tense when Aeric's teeth brush across my clit. Once, again, and a third time has me falling into the depths of pleasure. It washes over me in waves, threatening to pull me away. I might let it happen.

I'm shaking, unable to do anything but let it have me. It goes on for what feels like forever, the ecstasy and magic splashing up and through, one feeding the other and back again.

Aeric doesn't stop, using that infernal mouth to guide me through it and keep the pleasure going until I'm limp and gasping. Only then does he release me, still pressing kisses to the insides of my thighs. I'm glad that it's dark, so he can't see the way I'm blushing. It's been a long time since I've let anyone taste me, and I would have told him he didn't have to — that his hand would have worked just fine — had I been able to truly speak.

Light forms around us in a hazy cloud, pale and soft and dim. Just enough so that I can see him clearly, and he can see me. He's looking down at me now, not hiding the fact that he's taking me in. I imagine what I must look like for him — nightgown bunched up under my breasts, legs wantonly spread, pussy wet from his tongue.

The fire in his dark eyes makes me wish he hadn't stopped. That his mouth was still on me, tongue still inside me, making me come again and again. Instead, he kisses me on the mouth, hard body lowering to cover mine.

I can taste myself on his lips, rich and sweet. Aeric sweeps his tongue across mine, plunging deeper to take the kiss that he wants. *Yes*. Everything in me surges to meet him. I'm wet again and my nipples ache with need.

His hands find mine again, interlacing our fingers and raising them up so they're above my head. The way he's pressed up against me, I can feel how hard he is. He did want this. He might want more. But maybe not. I'll take whatever he wants to give.

"Thank you," I say when he pulls back for a moment.

"You're welcome." I feel the words in my gut.

I swallow, looking up at him. I'm trying to decipher the look on his face. It's unreadable. So I speak first. "You could have done less. Just the basics. Brae used his hand, and it worked just as well."

He raises an eyebrow, half of his mouth tipping into a lazy smile. "And why would I want to do that?" He kisses me long and slow, enough that my temperature rises, and I curl my legs around his hips. I'm practically begging for more. "You taste like sugar," he murmurs. "And roses. I've been dying to taste you."

"You wanted to?" I need to be sure.

He looks at me, and I realize that he doesn't have a shirt on. I was too lost in my own pleasure to see that before. But in this pool of light he's created I explore him with my eyes. Perfect chest and shoulders that I want to touch and trace—if he weren't pinning me to the bed. I try to move my hands, but he doesn't let me, intentionally gripping my wrists and keeping them there. "That and more," he says.

My heart skips a beat. "Are you just trying to save my life?"

Aeric slowly shakes his head, leaning down to press his lips to the bare skin of my shoulder.

"Do you want me because Brae had me first? Or do *you* want me?"

Aeric moves his hips, pressing his cock harder against me so I can feel it. Nothing but the thin fabric of his trousers separates us, and the pressure sends tingling sparks through me. His mouth slips up my neck, leaving a trail of shivers behind it, all the way to my ear where he can whisper. "This is not the way I would have chosen," he says, voice soft and fervent. "But I want you like I've wanted no other woman. And I have finished ignoring fate."

I'm not sure what that means, but my anxiety eases. He wants me. I can feel the truth of it in his body and in his gaze. "Okay," I say. "Thank you for helping me. I feel...wonderful."

"I sincerely hope it is not the last time," he says,

kissing me. It's a claiming kiss. Rough and deep. So thorough that it feels like a brand. I will never forget this kiss, and Aeric knows that. He presses further, until I forget where I am, and my own name. Words. I need the words.

Stay with me. Give me more. Take me. Fuck me. Where's my voice? "You can stay," I whisper.

"You need rest. Recovery," Aeric says, voice low.

The sound I make is needy. I don't want him to go. "I feel much better now."

He laughs, the vibrations in his chest rolling through me. "You might not if I stay. I would not stop," he whispers against my lips, "until you had no voice left with which to scream." Molten heat sinks straight to my core. God, yes. Please. "It would be worth it," I say.

"Yes, it would. Goodnight, Kari." With a final press of his lips on mine he's gone, the door shutting quietly behind him.

"Goodnight," I say to the empty air, the glow around me fading and the feel of his lips on mine still vivid in my mind. How in the hell am I going to be able to sleep now?

CHAPTER SEVENTEEN

KARI

In the morning I discover what I hadn't noticed last night—I've been given real clothes. Supple pants and shirts that seem sturdy and fit perfectly. They're a shade of deep forest green. I have no doubt that these are the clothes that Kaya was talking about making. As much as I loved the dress she made, it feels amazing to be wearing something closer to normal.

I'm not nearly as exposed, and if we're attacked again, I feel like I might be able to help. I can sense the magic in the fabric, even though I can't grasp the details. There are wards here.

Of course, after I told them what happened, she would weave protection into the clothing. I really hope I have the chance to thank her. Or see her again at all. Merina too. They were lovely, and in better circumstances I could see us being fast friends.

There's a bag as well, and I pack the spare clothes in it, as well as that little shimmering box that they gave me. It's not the box that makes me flush; it's the memory of last night and Aeric. It's enough to warm me and even consider the possibility of seeking him out this morning.

I put the flimsy nightgown in my bag too. If there's a chance that I can use it again, I'm going to.

There's a soft knock at my door, and I answer it. The Rialoia of the Crystal Court stands there, wearing clothes that seem out of place for a ruler. She's wearing something almost like my new clothes. Very casual and comfortable, though hers are a vivid blue that reminds me of pictures of the Caribbean. "I trust I did not wake you?"

"No, Rialoia."

"You may call me Nissa," she says, smiling. "I came to accompany you to the temple. Your companions have already been informed."

Right. She asked if she could see my attacker. And after last night, I'm inclined to agree. The more people know about her, the better. "Of course."

I leave the bag and follow her. We walk through twisting hallways of white stone, and there are so many that I don't remember which way is up or down. I was right though, the palace is a completely new experience in the daylight. The jeweled windows cast patterns on walls, creating images with light. Some are stories, history, and some are just beautiful.

We come to the large hallway that we crossed last night to get to the throne room, and the walls are filled with color—a perfect canvas for the artistry. This is clearly a story. There are images of war and death, pleasure and redemption, with one female figure central to it all.

In the image painted by the light streaming through the largest of the windows, the dark-haired woman is being torn apart by fire and light. And in the next she's entombed in glass like Snow White with four figures looking on, but the rest of the story is more colorful. No more war or bloodshed.

"What is this story?"

The Rialoia—Nissa—I correct myself, looks wistfully at the images. "It is how the Goddess saved Allwyn."

She doesn't elaborate, and the way she continues quietly contemplating the images before us tells me that is something deeply personal. I'll have to ask more later. Maybe one of the men will be willing to fill me in while we travel.

We cross into the open light outside of the

palace, and everything is just as vibrant, if not more so. The sky above us is deeply violet, and the buildings shine like pearls. For the first time since being in Allwyn I notice that there is no sun. The sky is filled with brilliant light, but I can't find the source.

Nissa is watching me, smiling in amusement. "We do not have day and night here like you do in the human realm on earth. Here it is simply the bright and the fade."

I look up at the sky again. In my life, I'd never considered that the sun was something you could take for granted. And yet it seems like I did. "How can you tell what time it is without the sun? Or the seasons?"

Nissa walks closer to the opal temple, which shimmers in the...I guess I can't call it daylight. But it's even more beautiful, with the colorful flecks changing and shifting as we approach. The rose is bigger than I realized, on an even greater scale. I feel tiny in comparison, and yet that same draw that filled me yesterday is present, telling me to come inside.

"Time," says Nissa, "is a very human concept. It does not pass in the same way. The bright and the fade never change. Neither do we have seasons, except in their own courts."

I blink. That's hard to wrap my mind around. "That's strange to me."

"And it would be to most humans, I imagine. That is not to say that we do not keep track of time in our own way. Like humans, we have cycles that repeat for celebrations and natural growth. But these things vary. Allwyn tells us when it is time."

We've reached the door of the temple, a large rectangular arch that is stark and open, simply cut into the stone. It contrasts against the rest of the building, which doesn't seem to have a straight line in it.

A fae female in a pale dress bows to Nissa and leads us inside. As soon as I cross the threshold, I feel the air change. Everything goes still, both inside and out. Peaceful.

It reminds me of water with no ripples. There's something there and hidden, ready to make waves. And the stillness only makes the presence more apparent.

Inside, the rose structure is open to the sky, though you couldn't see that from the outside, and it's no longer opal. It rather matches what the inside of a rose might look like, with shades of pinks and reds flowing one into another on the curved petal walls.

There doesn't seem to be any strict structure for

worship the way there is in human churches. In the center of the open space is one statue, formed from the same opal as the outside of the temple. The image is familiar.

The beautiful woman caught up in fire, but her face is utterly at peace. She's even smiling a little as she's consumed by the flames. It's striking, and a chill rolls through me. But other than the statue, there's nothing. No altars, no pews, nothing that made it clear where you where or what you were supposed to do.

There are cushions scattered across the polished jewel floor, and there are a few fae using them, heads bowed in silent prayer. Others are laying down, and still more are simply walking. It seemed like whatever form your worship wanted to take was allowed. The idea was freeing. Even though I'm not familiar with Allwyn's Goddess, the peace and safety that I feel here is enough that I almost don't want to leave.

Nissa leads us directly to the base of the statue where there is a sea of cushions spread across the floor, and we sit together, waiting. I don't feel the need to speak, just resting in that perfect silence. I'm trying to remember the last time that I felt this safe, and nothing is coming to mind. Even from long before the attack.

From the angle we're sitting at, the Goddess's face is nearly obscured by the statues fire, but I can see her smile. It seems crazy to feel like she's smiling at me, but I do.

A fae male approaches, dressed in the same kind of pale and flowing clothing as the acolyte at the gate. He looks normal. Almost human in coloring and body. His most remarkable feature is the vivid pink of his eyes. A simple silver band rests on his forehead, and he nods to Nissa. "Rialoia."

She nods in return and gestures to me. "Lai, this is Kari."

Lai kneels in front of me, looking at me in a way that feels like he's seeing through me. "Welcome to Allwyn, Kari," he says. "My Rialoia tells me you have a memory she would like to see."

I nod. "Yes. More than one. I'll show her everything I can."

He reaches out and stops. "I'll need to place my hand on you. Is that all right?"

I nod, and he puts a hand on my shoulder, and one on Nissa's as well. The magic that I feel is incredibly different than the ones I've felt before. It's a calm, slow, pulse. Like a heartbeat. It doesn't strive to arouse or to harm. It just exists.

It feels like that's all there is, and I could fade

away into that pulsing lull. "Kari," Lai says, though his voice sounds far away, "Please show us."

Right. I'm supposed to show them *her*. I think back to the time when she first came into the shop for that potion, and I just remember. I show them making the potion, the burst of magic that came in the creation and giving her the bottle. Then I skip forward to her calling my name and the attack. I'm not exactly sure if what I'm remembering is everything, but now that the memory is playing, the magic is guiding me. It coaxes the reality from memory without sending me into a spiraling panic.

I relive other things too. The worst of the pain and the attack with the birds. The first part of last night where my chest was glowing red, and I knew again that I was going to die.

But I'm removed from it all. I don't feel the pain in my body, and I know that I am safe here. Finally, the magic guides me back to the first memory, where her face is clear, and it focuses there. Until the magic slips away quietly and easily, and I open my eyes.

Lai removes his hand from my shoulder and looks over at Nissa. "Is that enough, Rialoia?"

She nods sharply, the set of her jaw telling me that she wasn't happy with what she witnessed. "I do not recognize this female," she says softly. "But if she enters the borders of the Stone Kingdom or the Crystal Court, she will not leave it."

Her conviction is fierce, and Lai's face shows the same passion. "Why?" The word flies from me before I can consider it.

"I am aware that not everyone in Allwyn values human life," Nissa says to me. "Perhaps some would even agree that this fae's assault on you was justified to take what she wanted. But our Goddess valued life—all life—so much she gave her own. I will not allow attacks on the innocent in my Court."

More than everything else I've experienced, the Court here has been turning my mind upside down. Everything is different from what I would have thought. But of course it is. You can't assume you know everything about a culture or people based on the stories that you're told. But when that's all you know, that's all you're able to expect.

But it's still astonishing to have so many strangers care about what happens to you. I can't say that the same thing would happen back in New York. "Thank you." Lai is staring at me strangely now, and I feel the urge to look away. But I can't. "Is something wrong?"

"Not at all," he says, hesitating. "But know this: the Goddess is not one of coincidence."

I swallow, those words sending a chill down my spine. "What does that mean?"

"I can't see the future," Lai says. "No one can. But no matter the unfortunate circumstances, you are meant to be here." He stands, and makes a short bow to Nissa, "I wish you well on your journey."

And he's gone before I can ask him if he means that I'm meant to be in Allwyn, or specifically in the Crystal Court. Whether it means I'm on the right path to be healed, or if entering this temple today was where I should be. Questions churn in my gut, and I no longer feel as peaceful.

Nissa places a hand lightly on my arm. "I'm sure your companions are waiting for us. The faster you make it to the Carnal Court, the more quickly you can be free of this curse."

She helps me to my feet and we exit the temple. Outside, the men are waiting along with the Rialoir, and there are fae horses. These are the animals Aeric spoke to me about. They look like horses you would see in the human world, but they're vibrant. The first horse I see looks like fire, yellow and orange and red flowing across its body.

The other horses are just as beautiful, a living rainbow, waiting and saddled as the men speak quietly.

Nissa presses her hand to my arm. "I believe

that Lai is right. You are meant to be here. When you are well, I hope to see you again, Kari."

"Thank you," I say. "For your kindness."

Her smile is brilliant. "Stay alive. That is your repayment."

"I'll do my best," I say, laughing.

As we approach the group, the men notice me. And the first one who does is Aeric. His dark hair shines in the light with a perfect green sheen, and he's smiling. Just a ghost of a smile, that's private for the two of us. "Good morning, Kari," he says quietly.

My face flames as the rest say their hellos. "Morning."

Kent guides me to the flaming horse, whose saddle holds my bag. "Are you all right?"

"I think so. No pain right now."

"Good." He leans forward and kisses me lightly, before retreating to his own horse which looks like it's made of the ocean.

Now that we're all here, we don't delay. Brae has a final few words with the rulers before we leave, drawing stares all the way out through the gates of the city.

CHAPTER EIGHTEEN

KARI

I rode a horse a few times when I was a teenager, but never since then. It's not particularly difficult, but I can already tell that I'm going to be sore.

We're moving much faster than when I had to be carried or share a horse, which is good. The scenery passing is strange and wonderful, and I'm grateful that I'm able to see it—sitting upright instead of through a haze of pain. Especially when I feel the first whisper of its return at mid-day.

Kent rides by my side, but says almost nothing. Which strikes me as strange. "You asked me if I was all right, but are you?"

"I'm fine," he says.

I look over and I see the tension in his shoulders and the set of his jaw. "You don't seem like it."

"I am."

"Okay." I don't think pushing him is going to help him open up, and he drifts away from me, riding ahead.

"How far away are we?" I ask, not directing the question to anyone in particular.

Brae looks back at me. "From the Carnal Court?"

I nod.

"A few days, at best. If we can keep up a good pace like this."

"Okay."

Verys's voice comes from behind me. "Are you worried?"

"Yes," the word is thick in my throat. "It seems to be moving faster."

Brae studies me for a moment. "It could be. You feel it already?"

As if in response to his question, a flare of nausea rises through my stomach. "It's not bad yet, but yeah."

"We'll be careful," Aeric says. "Go as fast as we can."

None of us are saying what the true worry is — that if this curse is speeding up, it might get to a point where we can't feed it enough magic to keep it at bay. But we all ride a little faster.

The day passes slowly, and when the light starts to fade, we find an alcove protected by an outcropping of yellow rock where we set up camp. The three fae males set up camp as if it's easy and natural, falling into established rhythms. They secure the horses and put my bag near the crystal cliff. Verys starts and controls a fire.

We were given bedding, as well as food and clothing. The camp already feels much better than before, even if we're caught in tense silence. I sit on the bedding that has been set out near the fire and eat the delicious bread that was sent with us. Part of me wonders if they somehow knew that this was my favorite part of last night's feast and included the bread and honey and jam for that reason.

Even if it wasn't on purpose, it's so good that I could eat it forever, just lost in the flavor. The rest eat in silence. We've been in that same silence for most of the day, consumed by our own thoughts. But now that we're not riding, the silence is loud. There are questions I want to ask them, but the time doesn't feel right.

The pain inside me has been rising since midday, growing to a consistent ache in my bones. It's so frustrating, knowing that it's constantly coming back. And after this morning in the temple, re-living all those memories, the biggest question I have is *why?*

Whether I'm supposed to be here or not, it doesn't explain why *me?* Why was I the target of this? Have there been others? Will there be more after me? After the curse is lifted—if it can be lifted—will she keep trying to come back? Will she keep trying to kill me?

My mind has been going in circles all day, retracing the same questions. I don't have answers. None of us do. But that doesn't mean my brain doesn't keep trying to solve the puzzle.

I finish the bread and brush the crumbs from my hands before stretching. My hips are sore from the ride, and I'm sure they'll be even worse tomorrow.

"Kari," Brae says from his seat across the fire. "Do you need pleasure?"

I go still.

Yes.

My brain immediately says it. But I stop the word flying towards my mouth before it can reach my lips. It's something I want, and yet I'm still not used to talking about it openly like that. But these fae are who they are. Sex and pleasure is a part of their lives. They have no reason to be coy about it.

"So you can make it through the night," Aeric says, referring to my episode in the castle.

Even if I didn't need it, I *want* it. I want to feel what pleasure with them is like when I'm not drowning in pain that's trying to kill me. It just happens that there's an added benefit of keeping the curse at bay.

Kent is staring into the fire beside Brae, and he hasn't reacted to their words, though he must have heard. I ache for him, too. I love him, and he loves me, and I know that watching someone else pleasure me is going to hurt him. I don't want that. But I can't deny the way I'm attracted to the fae men, and the fact that they can heal me is a factor. I want them. And him. Everything about this makes me conflicted.

Kent looks up from the fire and meets my eyes, and I see a rawness there that I haven't before. His gaze floats down the length of my body before circling back to my eyes. "Don't say no if I'm what's stopping you," he says.

"Are you sure?"

He huffs out a breath. "I'd rather see and hear anything than you in pain, Kari. Please."

He must have heard me screaming last night, and possibly more. Oh.

I wet my lips, breathing through my sudden anxiety. I want this, and I need it. But it's strange to ask, no matter if they've told me more than once to tell them what I need. Swallowing, I look at Brae, and then at Aeric. "Yes."

"I'll keep watch." Verys stands, stepping to the edge of the camp. Far enough away to be observant, but not so far that he won't be able to see and hear. I see him glance backwards from the edge of our camp with keen interest.

Brae stands and comes around the fire, pulling me to my feet. Seconds later I feel another body behind me, and Aeric's lips on my neck, his magic accompanying the kiss. "Both of you?"

"If the curse is escalating, we will too."

"Oh." Both of them. At the same time. The thought makes me immediately wet. I can feel my pulse everywhere in my body. Attraction, desire, pleasure. *Please.*

Brae's hands find the hem of my shirt and peel it easily over my head. His magic glows within me too, the two different powers shivering against each other. One a cool breeze, the other like sunlight. They're so different and yet they're working together. Just the feeling of the magic writhing and dancing beneath my skin is leaving goosebumps. My soul is reaching out, wanting to bask in the different lights of their energy.

Aeric's arms circle my waist, guiding me down onto the ground so I'm leaning against him. Hands roam my skin, across my ribs and up to my breasts. My nipples are already hard before he touches them, and when he rolls them through his fingers, my eyes fall closed. The sensation is amplified with magic, sending vibrations straight down to my pussy. Dear god, this more than I expected.

Brae strips my pants off in one easy movement, and I can't breathe. This is happening. Really happening.

Aeric whispers in my ear. "I can't wait to taste you again, Kari. Brae is lucky that I'm willing to share."

He squeezes my breasts again, making me moan, and Brae takes the opportunity to part my legs. Sunshine and light cascade into me when his mouth touches my skin. It's a storm of bright, sheer pleasure, entirely different from how Aeric pleasured me. Brae's tongue moves smoothly and precisely. Rolling waves and patterns that grow and fade in intensity, every time they reach their peak I think I might go over, but I don't. He keeps pulling me back down into that warm, hazy place where even the air I breathe feels *good*.

I manage to open my eyes, and Kent is watching us. His gaze is fierce, locked on mine. It takes a moment for me to realize what expression is on his face. Not anger, but jealousy.

Shock rolls through me, contrasting with my arousal, and I keep looking at Kent. His own arousal is plain to see, his pants tight enough to look painful. And the other half of his expression is agony. He wants me. He wants this. And he can't look away.

Brae pushes my legs further apart. He holds them there so I'm wide open and exposed as he plunges his tongue deep. *Fuck*. Sharp, exquisite need rises through me, leaving me breathless and writhing. And then he's just working my clit, sucking it between his lips. He's teasing and licking and humming and biting and I don't think I'll ever be able to breathe again.

Aeric gently bites my shoulder as he pinches my nipples. He's doing it on purpose and making me want more. It's working. I want everything. I can't stop the needy sounds coming out of my mouth, barely managing to bite my lips before I start begging Brae to go faster.

I look back to Kent, shocked by the naked lust in his eyes. Every muscle in his body is taught, ready to spring like he's about to fight. But it's not the fight he wants, it's me. Underneath me I can feel Aeric's cock hard as steel against my spine. He's aroused too, and I don't doubt that if I could see it,

Brae would be hard as well. This is impossible, and yet it's still happening.

Pale, mint green magic ripples down through my skin from Aeric's touch. It feels like he's stroking me from the inside, mixing with Brae's bright, sparkling flares and I come, shaking. "Oh my god," the words barely come out. "Fuck." My whole body is taught with the orgasm. I can't move, caught in the storm.

The magic soaks into me, erasing the ache and the pain, relieving me of the burden and letting me relax. "Again," Aeric says, but I'm not sure if it's to Brae or to me. It doesn't seem to matter, it has the same effect.

Brae toys with my clit with his fingers, every little motion making me shudder because it's so sensitive. Too sensitive and too much. "Brae," I breathe. *"Brae."* He doesn't stop, pleasures slicing through me with a razor edge. I catch Kent's eyes as I'm washed away by the second orgasm. He's my anchor in the storm of pleasure, those gray eyes helping me to let go and stay centered at once. For a moment I go blind with the pleasure, and then I'm back.

"One more," Brae says, his mouth crashing down on me again. He shifts my legs onto his shoulders so he can bury his mouth in me deeper, and I'm lost in all of it. Aeric's lips and tongue graze my neck, hands stroking and rolling my breasts hard. I'm already limp and sated, allowing their pleasure to swell and break over me again.

Kent's knuckles are white, locked together. I have an image of him stroking himself, and I want to see it. I want to watch him have pleasure too. Have him come with me.

It's that thought that sends me over the third time, pleasure ripping me into tiny pieces and putting me back together again. Any pain is a thing of the past. I sigh in contentment as Brae lowers my legs to the ground again. His lips are shiny with my wetness, and despite the three orgasms my pussy dampens again when he licks his lips, never taking his eyes off mine. Oh. Fucking. God.

"You both are too good at that."

Brae laughs. "Did you think Carnal Fae would give pleasure poorly?"

I shake my head, still trying to catch my breath. There's a thin sheen of sweet on my skin, and a waft of a breeze through the camp makes me shiver.

Aeric slips out from underneath my body, laying behind me. His arm is still around me so I'm trapped between the fire and the inferno of heat that is his body. "Tonight I won't leave you," he says. As if to prove it, his fingers graze my skin towards my pussy, which is still throbbing with need. I don't know how I can still want more. I think if they actually gave me more I might pass out. "In case you have need in the night."

I nod, my head laying on the bedding. I don't have the energy to speak, and if I did, I'm afraid that I would simply beg. Kent is still watching me, face now unreadable, pants still straining with arousal. I try to smile at him. It's weak, but it's there. He smiles back. Small. Just for me.

God, I'm exhausted. I want to keep looking at him. I want to be awake and to say thank you, but I'm sinking down through the floor and into sleep. Aeric pulls me tighter against his body, and I feel a kiss on my temple before I fade into slumber.

CHAPTER NINETEEN

BRAE

I watch Kari fall asleep in Aeric's arms, my cock so hard that it's aching. Her naked body is relaxed and peaceful, forced into ease by the pleasure we showed her. That was so much more than the first time. I can still taste her on my lips and Goddess, I could happily spend an eternity between her legs for more of that sweetness. I know that I'm never going to be able to rest while I'm this hard, so I step away from the fire and the sight of Kari's perfect sleeping form out past the circle of light and further. Around the corner of a rock formation, close enough to hear if I am needed.

Releasing my cock from my pants into my hand, I let the images that I've fought against rise up into my mind. Fought against because there are more important things than fantasizing when we could lose her. When we have to move fast. But for these few moments, she's safe.

I imagine her naked body under mine again, but this time not in pain. This time her eyes are vibrant and laughing and my name is on her lips, tortured and begging the way it was tonight. She grabs my hips as I line my cock up with that perfect pink cunt.

Last night when I heard Aeric pleasuring her, I listened and pleasured myself, but that was before I had tasted her and felt her shaking under my tongue. Goddess, I can almost feel what she'll be like when I sink myself into that heat. Perfect and soft, squeezing me in all the right ways.

Stroking myself, I let the pleasure flow up and over me, waking my magic and fueling it. I need it to help Kari, and I need this release. I picture her writhing underneath me, stretched on my cock, lips parted in perfect ecstasy. I want to be the cause of that look on her face every day.

Harder, I wring pleasure from myself, too aroused and too hard to last long. I watch her in my mind as she's overcome with pleasure, and I feel my balls tighten with the orgasm I seek, letting it explode from me, letting the magic pour into my veins, harnessing it and saving it, keeping it close. I sag against the stone, continuing to tease my cock through the pleasure as it fades.

Sweet relief, even if I'm still going to be hard as soon as I see her again, or as soon as I think about the taste of her climax. I've lived a long life, and not a chaste one, and I have tasted nothing better than Kari. Her flavor alone makes me want to worship her on my knees, and it's more than that. She is kind and vibrant, and even though we barely know each other, I *want* her. My very soul reaches for her.

But for now, I will content myself with the taste of her pleasure on my tongue. A taste I will never forget and which will never compare to anything else.

Just one more confirmation of what the three of us fae know and haven't admitted. That Kari—this beautiful, dying, human—is our mate.

It seems impossible, but there is no other explanation.

Sharing a female isn't uncommon in Allwyn. There are fewer of them and love finds its way where it will. The tangled webs of relationships in the Fae Realm would find no equal in the human world. But mates are rare enough that they are rarely shared. Being mated is all-consuming. A bond down to the core and magic of the fae involved.

I'd heard rumors a long time ago of someone who had more than one mate, but I thought it was just that. A story. Now, I have a mate, and she's *human* and so, so, fragile. And two others are her mates as well. At least.

How would Kari react to being told that we're her mates? It's clear that she wants us, and we want her. Even Verys, though he holds back. I walk back to our camp, holding the question in my mind. I do not want her to be afraid of what this means. I want her to welcome it with open arms. But she's lost so much already, I can't predict what she'll say or what she'll think.

Kari is still fast asleep, Aeric holding her. I see the way his fingers are touching her. Holding her as close as he dares without waking. His eyes are closed, but his body is alert. I doubt he'll get any sleep, pressed against her body like that. I wouldn't either, caught between desire and the need to protect her from what hunts her at all costs.

Kent is still sitting by the fire where I left him, staring at her sleeping form, but he looks up when I come closer. I nod away from them, not wanting to risk any sound that might disturb Kari's rest. To my surprise, he follows me without hesitation. We walk beyond the horses, to where we can speak without worry. "Are you all right?" I ask him.

I am curious. He has struggled with this, and I

empathize. The thought of Kari with someone else, other than those she's mated to, and this man who has loved her, makes me vibrate with a rage that I do not want to contain.

Kent crosses his arms and looks away into the distance. "I honestly don't know." I sense there's more, and I wait. After a minute, he sighs. "I've been in love with Kari for a long time. And when I thought I was going to lose her, nothing else mattered. And after everything, I thought that watching that would upset me."

He doesn't say anything else. I wonder how he feels if he wasn't upset by it? I reach out with my magic, not to touch him or affect him in any way, just to read him emotionally. But he is a blur. There's no clear reading, his thoughts and emotions are moving so quickly. Can I trust him now? He seems changed from when he tried to attack me, and when he threatened to come after us. "Is your plan still to hunt us down after Kari is healed?"

"No," he lets out a breath. "You three—and those at the Crystal Court—have been showing me that not all fae are what I thought they were. Or what I have experienced. It's been...eye opening to see that what you've believed for so long might not be true." He doesn't elaborate on the experiences that formed those beliefs, and now is not the time to ask. That much is clear. But I can tell that his anger towards us is extinguished, and that's good enough for me.

"I," I say, "and the others. We feel a connection to Kari. We care about her. Far more than we should for a random human that we encountered." I don't tell him that this terrifies us, or that he'll never know how desperate it makes us to save her life.

He goes very still. Not in anger, not preparing for a fight. Just suddenly at attention. "What does that mean?"

"To be sure, I must get back to my Court." I do not want to tell him we are mates. Not yet. His anger is gone, but that kind of possession will not be easy to swallow. "But you should know that we do not want to lose her."

Kent nods shortly.

"You should also know that this is not uncommon."

"What isn't?"

I glance back towards the fire. "Sharing a female."

Kent's expression goes slack, and then to awe, and then unreadable again. It seems I've handed him a revelation that he doesn't know what to do with yet. Or how he feels about it. I'm not sure either, because this is all new to me. I never thought

I would be granted a mate. It wasn't a part of my plan. In fact, it changes my life a lot. But I wouldn't take it back. Not even for a second.

One thing remains. The thing that makes my gut clench and my muscles go stiff. If any of this is going to matter, then Kari has to survive.

CHAPTER TWENTY

KARI

*P*leasure crashes down on me in a crushing wave, washing away what's left of the pain and leaving me wrecked against Brae's chest. The pain was bad today, with agony creeping up on me by the time we stopped for the night. Or fade, as I've started to call it.

I lean my head back, taking deep breaths and enjoying the teasing of Brae's fingers as he brings me down. He's hard behind me, cock pressing into my ass. They've never asked me for any reciprocation in pleasure, though I know they would be open to it. It feels like I've had more orgasms in the last few days than I've had in the past few years, and I can't deny that I'm enjoying it even if it is for a terrible reason.

Not only does it bring me relief, but these men

know how to make my body *sing*. They pull pleasure from places I didn't know it could exist. Not to mention they're sexy. I've spent a fair share of time pressed to their bodies as they master mine, and though Aeric is the only one I've gotten a glimpse of, I can feel that they're exquisite.

Verys hasn't touched me yet, but he wants to. He watches, burning heat in his gaze, each moment coming closer.

I open my eyes now to find Kent's gaze locked on mine. He's standing at the edge of our camp, that same mix of arousal and longing on his face that I've seen him have for three days now. But every time I try to talk to him, he's quiet and withdrawn. That ends now. "Brae," I say softly. "I need Kent tonight." Meaning that I want him to lay with me. Because we've come too far for him to disappear on me now.

"Very well," he says, pulling me close for a moment before standing. He doesn't seem bothered by my request, though I might be hurt if the situation were reversed. Everyone has seemed very okay with it. Which is surprising and utterly amazing. My mind flies back to the conversation with Merina and Kaya. Sharing a partner is normal here.

I motion to Kent, and he looks surprised, but he comes over. I pat the bedding beside me, and he lays down with me. He's hard already from watching me with Brae. I can feel it.

He puts his hand on my waist gently, almost like he's afraid to touch me. But as soon as our skin connects he pulls me to him, and I relax, breathing him in. He smells like familiar memories, wood and rain and fog. Tucking my head into his chest, I let him hold me.

"I miss you," I say softly into his shirt.

Kent's fingers tighten on my skin like a reflex. "I miss you too."

"You don't talk to me," I say.

"There's too much to say." His other hand curls underneath me, weaving into my hair to hold me even closer.

I shake my head, curling into him. "We've never had trouble talking. You always talked to me on bad days. You made me feel better."

"I'm sorry, Kari."

I look up at him, our faces close. Having him this close, being nearly naked with him, it's everything I've wanted with him for so long. But over the past two days, only Brae and Aeric have touched me. It's been amazing and delicious, and I might be selfish, but I want Kent too. "Why haven't you touched me?"

Kent stares at me, and he swallows but doesn't speak.

"I can see that you want to. I want you to."

Gently, he pulls my mouth to his. It's slow, and steadily deepening. This kiss sinks down into my stomach and makes me ache. Every one of these men means something to me now. But Kent has been in my life the longest, and he's seen me at my lowest point. My life would be very different if we had never met. He's been my anchor, and my heart aches when I think of ever being apart.

Kent brushes his tongue across my lips, and I open to him. I kiss him harder, pressing closer and wrapping my arms around him until we're too tangled up in each other to know where one or the other ends.

"You know I've always wanted you, Kari. From the first moment I saw you. It's even more than that. I love you. I hope you know that."

My breath catches in my chest. "Still?"

"I never stopped loving you. Wanting you. I don't even mind if I have to share you."

An unexpected smile bursts onto my face. "Really?"

Kent laughs under his breath. "Really. I don't know why I find it so hot, but I do."

"I like it when you watch me," I tell him. His

eyes on me while they've been pleasuring me have made it that much better.

"I'm serious, Kari," he says. "I can't believe that I'm saying this, but I see the way you look at them. And it's the same way that you look at me. I'll share you. I'll do whatever you want. But I'm never going to leave you." He kisses me again, leaving me completely melted under his attention.

When he pulls away I have to drag my eyes open, lulled by the addicting nature of his kiss. "That doesn't explain why you haven't touched me," I say.

"I'm touching you now."

"Kent—"

"I don't have magic," he says, answering. "Touching you, giving you pleasure, no matter how much I'm dying to, doesn't help you."

I shake my head, pressing my lips against his softly. "I think you and I have different definitions of help."

"I'm talking about keeping you alive. I can't lose you."

"You're not going to lose me," I say. "Right now I feel *good*. And I want to feel good with you. Or if you want, I'll make you feel good. I can feel how much you want me."

"You don't have to," he says, but I'm already

moving downwards. I want to. I want to show him how I feel with pleasure. I want to know what he tastes like after all this time dying to know. Kent groans as I release his cock from his pants, and every fantasy I've ever had about this moment comes flooding to my mind.

He's hard and thick, filling up my hand. I like the way he feels under my fingers, and he groans when I stroke up the length of his shaft. "Kari," my name sounds like both a curse and a prayer on his lips.

I touch my lips to the tip of him, letting him slide into my mouth, and the sound he makes sends heat rushing down through my core. My pussy dampens in response. It's used to being aroused, and this is no exception to that rule.

Kent's hand is still gripping my hair, and his fingers tighten when I dive down onto him, taking him as far as I can into my mouth. There was a time when I thought that this would never happen, and now we're here and I love the way it feels.

Releasing him briefly, I drag my tongue from base to tip. His cock jerks, and he curses under his breath. I smile, kissing my way down to his balls and back. Slowly, so slowly, I seal my mouth to his skin and suck to the tip of his cock, teasing him. I push down onto his shaft an inch at a time, pulling back with each stroke and taking him further. Until he's filling my mouth completely, cock bumping the back of my throat and I'm straining to contain him.

Pulling back, I dive back down onto him again. I take him almost completely, and he groans. Both of his hands wind into my hair and pull me firmly onto his cock. My lips touch the skin of his stomach and Kent curses again. His cock jumps in my throat, and I swallow him.

Kent thrusts his hips once, again, and a final time, crying out my name as he spills himself down my throat. He tastes of salt and something deeper. I want all of it. All of him. I hold myself hard against him, not releasing him until he's finished and I've swallowed everything that he has to give.

When he looks down at me, his eyes are glazed with pleasure. He doesn't seem remotely bothered by the fact that we had an audience. Hauling me upwards along his body, Kent pins me to the bedding and puts his lips to my skin. Finally, finally, he's touching me.

A dam has been unleashed. Everything that has been held back is released, and I'm overwhelmed by it. Kent worships my body. Thoroughly. My breasts swell under his attention. The path he traces with his tongue leaves fire on my shuddering skin. By the time he's between my legs I'm already half-way there.

Scratch that, I'm all the way there. The second his tongue touches my clit my orgasm hits. Deep, swirling, pleasure swells and pulls me under the wave of it. Kent covers me with his mouth, sucking relentlessly. It sends me over again, my body falling into the rhythm it now knows thanks to the past few days—coming over and over again. Nothing but a haze of delicious and sweet feelings roll through me until it's over.

Kent is over me now, kissing me without reservation or shyness. Not caring at all that I've already been touched by another male tonight. I love him for that. I love when he helps me pull on my clothes because the temperature has dropped in the Kingdom of Stone and it's too cold for me to sleep naked with him. I love when he wraps me in his arms and holds me close, tangling us together so we can fall asleep. Finally, together.

CHAPTER TWENTY-ONE

KARI

I open my eyes to white. Purely the color. I blink, trying to clear away whatever glare has blinded me, but there's nothing. I'm colder than I remember being when I fell asleep, and I can feel that Kent's arms are not around me anymore. I reach for him, but I can't reach for him, because I can't move.

I can't move.

I can't open my mouth to scream. Nothing in my body is responding, not even when I try to make any kind of sound. All that does is raise the taste of thick, burnt ash and rotting fruit, and bring back the memory of blooming pain. No. No. *No.*

My stomach spirals into sick dread. No. This can't be happening. I was safe. I was *safe*. I was surrounded by protection. She can't be here. This is a dream and I have to wake up. Now.

Please. I beg anyone, any God or Goddess who will listen. *Get me out of here.*

My vision suddenly clears, and I'm surrounded by white again but I can see now. The white is stone. It looks icy and menacing. I'm still in the Kingdom of Stone, but this is not a place I have seen before. I have no idea how far I have been taken. Do they know I am gone yet?

Oh my god, they won't know where I am. I can see them now, realizing that I'm gone and what it must mean and it makes my chest ache. The strange, white stone landscape blurs with the tears in my eyes, and I blink them away, ignoring the grieving hole in my chest. I need to focus. I need to find a way back to them. It's not fair. They've worked so hard to keep me alive. I can't let it happen like this. I will not die here.

I can see enough to know that I'm floating, suspended in the air. I don't feel weightless, but I'm not touching anything. In the absolute corners of my vision I can see two figures, cloaked and shrouded with outstretched hands. Flickers of magic fly out from them. They're what's keeping me afloat.

My heart stops when she steps into my line of vision. *Her*. The fae female who's tried to kill me twice now. She looks almost the same as I remember. Long, pale blonde hair flows over her shoulders. Perfect features and dark eyes. She's stunningly beautiful. Gone is the dark dress from when she first attacked me, replaces with simpler clothing, close to what I'm wearing.

She stares me in that way that I remember, looking down at me with mild curiosity. Her head tilts to the side as she studies me, barely a flicker in her expression as she studies me.

"So strange, that a human would cause so much trouble," she says softly. "You have enough magic to steal, but certainly aren't worth the protection of three fae warriors. So what is it that I have failed to notice about you?"

I still can't move, but this time, when I try to speak, I can. Barely. My voice is low and raspy, like it's being forced through whatever magic is binding me. "You wanted to steal my magic?"

A condescending smile, just for a moment. "I imagine that at this point you are wondering who I am."

I am, but I don't say anything. She probably won't answer any questions that I ask, regardless.

"My name is Ariana," she continues, looking down at me. "But that is all you shall ever know."

"Please, just tell me why?" I'm desperate.

She reaches out and traces a finger down my cheek. "You are so interesting. It's a pity I cannot afford to indulge my curiosity."

"Tell me why," I say again.

"You are rare." Her gaze runs down my body in an appraising way, all the way to my feet and circling back to meet my eyes. "Humans who are born with magic. So old, so diluted. So different from Allwyn's magic. And I have need of it."

It's both relieving and horrifying to know that it has nothing to do with me. There's nothing I could have done to prevent this. It's just a quirk, handed down from however many generations ago that a fae was in my family line.

But even though there's nothing I could have done to stop it, there's nothing I did to attract it either. Which is just so monumentally unfair. It was random. Could have been anyone. Might have already been. "Were there others?"

"Yes," she says, her eyes devoid of emotion. "Do you find that comforting?"

I shudder in spite of the magic paralyzing me. "No."

She raises her hand, examining a blood-red crystal in her fingers. It glows like a coal, and I already know that it's infused with the same magic I've been feeling all this time, the curse she cast that's been slowly killing me. That wasn't meant to last this long at all. "Of all of them, know that you lasted the longest. That alone makes you different." A twitch of her lips. "I know how much humans desire to be different."

Suddenly the magic that's holding me tightens, constricting to the point of pain and I can't breathe. Her fingers wrap around my jaw, forcing it open with one hand while she drops the crystal into my mouth with the other. She shoves it towards my throat, and I retch, whole body stinging with the pressure of magic and pain of invasion.

Forcing my mouth closed, one hand wraps over my nose and mouth, cutting off all possibility of breath. "Swallow it."

I shake my head the fraction of an inch it will move. I try to make myself react. To spit. To force this piece of stone away from me, but I can't. Nothing works. Except I can breathe, if she'd let me. And swallow.

The crystal's magic is already burning, seeping into the skin of my mouth and spreading pain outward and down to the rest of me. I won't. I won't do it. But I'm quickly running out or air, and the minute I try to take a breath I know what's going to happen. I won't die like this. I *can't* die like this. Not alone.

Tears rush to my eyes again, spilling over and down my skin. I see Ariana look at them, and she doesn't react. I knew, deep down, that she wouldn't react. But it hurts anyway. She sees me as nothing. As less than nothing. She's going to dump my body for them to find like I've never existed.

Oh my god, I'm never going to see them again. A new wave of tears flows and pain rips through my chest. They mean something to me. Every one of them. More than the sex and the fact that they saved my life. Something has been pulling us together, and it's shattering. I've never felt so broken.

I'm out of air, but I don't breathe. I hold on until I'm dizzy with the lack of it. If this bitch wants to kill me, I'm not going to make it easy. She's still watching me, and she smiles, just a little. Like she knows I'm determined to fight with whatever I've got.

Air. I need it. Crave it. There are spots in my vision. The world is dark and spinning. I don't have a choice but to take a breath. But I can't. Her hand is sealed over my nose and mouth, blocking it. There's more than a hand there—there's power. Cutting me off from every supply. My body is convulsing, begging for anything even though there's nothing to take. I inhale anyway—or try—gulping empty atmosphere trying to stay alive.

I realize my mistake too late when the crystal slips down my throat, burning its way through my chest and deep down. It's lodged there, churning fire and spitting pain like I've swallowed lit gasoline.

Her hand leaves and air flies into my lungs so fast it makes me choke. Light and color come back, and so does the pain that was dimmed by my dying. It's never felt like this before. Pure. Acute. Distilled.

And then she puts her hand on my chest, and everything explodes. My vision fades to white, and I recall this sensation with shocking clarity. I'm back on the sidewalk in New York, and my life is being pulled away. I feel it moving inside me, gladly running to her as she calls it. This time there's no coming back.

There's a sound, like slithering. Slow and steady and shivering. I can smell the burning of orange peels, and I remember what this looks like. Her crimson magic stealing the colors of my soul, even though I can't see it.

And of course, there's the pain. She's ripping me to bits, methodically separating my soul from my bones. I'm being ground to dust and blown away. The white behind my eyes is fading to gray. She's lit me on fire, hasn't she? She must have, if I feel this way.

I've always wondered what it would feel like to

burn alive. What it would be like to be one of those martyrs burned at the stake. Now I understand.

I would have chosen any other way to go, but under the circumstances…

dissolving…

seems like

a mercy

CHAPTER TWENTY-TWO

KENT

I reach for Kari and feel nothing. She must have shifted away in the night. I reach further, but there's still nothing. Cracking open one eye, she's not lying next to me anymore. It's possible that she just stepped away to relieve herself, but the bedding beside me is stone cold.

I'm fully awake now, scanning the camp. Aeric is nowhere, but Brae and Verys are sleeping by the low fire. "Kari," I say, at a normal volume. If she's around the corner, I don't want to panic. But there's something inside me that tells me she's not close, and there's no answer.

"Brae, Verys," I say louder. Their eyes open, and then like I did, they shift instantly into alertness.

"Where is she?" Brae asks.

I swallow. "I don't know."

I've never seen anyone move so fast. They're on their feet in seconds, buckling on the weapons they carry with them and are sprinting out of the camp. I'm with them too. "Kari!" I shout it as loud as I can in case she's somewhere close. I want to be wrong. *Please let me be wrong.*

I'm not wrong.

Outside the circle of our camp is a crumpled body. Aeric. He's unconscious and bleeding from a wound in his side, but he's still breathing.

My entire body goes cold. She was taken while she was *right next to me*. I didn't hear anything, didn't even wake. Fuck. How could this have happened? Fierce, nauseating terror grips me, and I have to breathe. Shove it down. Fear isn't going to get her back.

But I know it's not going away. I love Kari. She's it for me. It's the end of the story. It doesn't matter if I'm sharing her with ten men; she will always be the love of my life. I can't lose her. Not now.

Brae places his hand over Aeric's wound and it seals together. It's not fully healed, but enough to stop the damage. Aeric jerks like he's been electrocuted, thrashing before he comes awake coughing. "Aeric," Brae says. "What happened?"

He's still coughing, but he sits up. "I didn't see anything. One blast. Came out of nowhere, and I was down." He spits onto the ground. "Dark magic. I've never felt anything like that before. Except in New York."

"Can you move?"

Aeric stands, wincing. "Like hell are you going without me. I'm fine."

"Give me a weapon," I say. The three of them turn to me in unison, like they forgot I was there for a moment.

Verys looks at me. "Maybe you should hang back. This isn't something you've dealt with." That's code for 'you'll be in the way.' I'm not having that right now.

"I've killed fae before," I say flatly.

They're all staring at me still, and the energy shifts with the new information. I have killed fae before, and no, I'm not going to tell them about it. Aeric steps forward and unsheathes a wicked-looking knife from his belt and hands it to me. "Let's go."

We take nothing with us but the essentials. We can always come back once we find her. Or—

I stop the thought in its tracks. We are going to find her. Alive.

Verys takes the lead, and the other two allow it. I don't question it, assuming that he some sort of tracking skill that will help us. I keep looking around for any sign of her, but we're in a place with no brush. No plant-life or dirt. Nothing that I would normally use to track someone.

But Verys walks without hesitation. And then he stops, tilts his head. I can see from here that his eyes are closed, like he's listening to something. "There." His eyes snap open, and he points to the left. All of us start to sprint. There's no time and we all know it, but we can't say it out loud.

I feel the desperation in my companions and it is equal to mine. We won't lose her. We can't.

The scenery changes as we run. The color vanishes out of the landscape, fading into paler stone. The formations that once had vibrant streaks of purples, blues, and yellows are now entirely white. Were it not for the violet sky I would think we were in Antarctica. There's a small breeze whistling through the stones, and the cold scent of dust and emptiness.

Suddenly I'm running alone. All three fae stand frozen behind me, Brae falling to his knees and vomiting. Aeric is heaving in breaths and looks positively ill, and Verys is stock still, eyes like fire with a gaze on the horizon.

"What is it?"

"Black magic," Brae grits out. "Bad."

Verys locks eyes with me. "But we know exactly where she is."

There is nothing else to be said. Brae shoves himself up from the ground, and we're running now with Verys leading the way. Spires of white stone rise up around us like fangs, stark and sinister.

Anxiety churns in my gut. We're close now. Please, please let her be alive.

There's a cluster of rock formations up ahead and the fae next to me speed up. I can't keep up with them, but I push myself as hard as my body can go. They make it first, disappearing behind the rocks. I'm seconds behind them, and I see them clearing the area behind the stones, searching for enemies.

And then I see Kari.

What's left of her.

Red, curling magic writhes in serpentine shapes over her body. Her skin has gone flat and white, along with her hair. The life has been leeched out of her. I fall to my knees beside her, gather her up into my arms without a thought. Her skin is cold like the stone beneath her.

My stomach plummets into despair. No. No. But there, just the tiniest shift in her chest. A breath? "Kari." I whisper to her, even though my voice breaks. "Kari, please. Don't let go. Come back."

Terror as sheer as a cliff drives through me. If she's alive, there's a chance. But we might be too late. And I can do nothing.

Then Brae is there with me, banishing this magic with a blast of his own. His hands cup Kari's face, and he places his forehead against hers.

The words are like rocks in my mouth, but I have to know. "Is she gone?"

"Almost."

Light pours from his hands into Kari's chest, bright as the sun. He doesn't hold back. And I hold on to her. I don't want to let go. This tiny hope is all I have right now. Kari is the center of everything, and I don't know what to do if she doesn't come back.

CHAPTER TWENTY-THREE

KARI

"*K*ari." The voice sounds very far away. It caresses my mind like a whisper.

"Kari, please. Don't let go. Come back." Words slither softly in the darkness. I'm blind, but I can sense the empty expanse around me. This doesn't make me afraid, even though I'm standing on the edge of a cliff. No, the fall will be invigorating. This blackness is comforting. There's nothing to fear here. Why would I leave?

"Is she gone?" the whispers sound anguished. I used to know what that meant. A flicker of something deep inside—something I should remember but do not.

"Almost."

But I'm not gone. I'm right here. Who are these whispers?

Light as bright as the sun burns through the darkness. Pain and brilliance and *life*. My soul climbs out of the darkness and back into my body. But I don't want it. There's nothing but pain. I open my eyes to violet sky. Faces float over mine, and the first breath I take is like inhaling an inferno. Every cell craves more oxygen and there's not enough. My own body is fighting itself for air.

I can hear them speaking, voices relieved, but their words don't make sense. Muffled. Not penetrating the fog around my mind. Brae. That's who's speaking to me.

He's beautiful. I want to reach out and touch him, but my body will not move. Not because I'm bound, but because of weakness. I don't have the strength. I'm trapped inside myself.

That light that burns is his magic. The sunny, happy feeling that I'm starting to remember has turned hard and biting. Ruthless. Unyielding. It's bringing me back. Trying to. I am not all the way there. This, I know.

"Brae." I try to say it, but my lips don't move the way I tell them to. They're too busy gasping for breath. I'm outside of myself, and I don't like the feeling. Things are flooding back to fast. It's dizzying.

Ariana. She killed me, or tried. Focus. I'm lying on hard stone. Brae is hovering over me, speaking. His eyes are the green of the jungle we traveled through. His lips are moving, his voice slowly becoming clearer.

"You need more," he says. The words still fuzzy, but I can understand them. Warmth seeps into my skin where he touches me. Palms pushing my shirt off my shoulders. Other hands lift it over my head. "More than I can give you my mouth or my hands. Kari, if you're in there, I need you to give me a sign. Any kind of sign."

Fingers graze my hips, tracing down the bare skin of my legs. Other hands too. He's removing my pants. Oh. *Oh*. A sign. He needs me to say yes. Because we've never done this before.

I try to move again, but I get nothing more than a flicker from my fingers or toes. Frustration curls up inside my chest. There has to be away. I came back. They brought me back, but I can feel myself slipping. I'm not going to leave them again just because they couldn't hear me.

Closing my eyes, I think. It feels so easy to keep them closed.

Open your eyes.

I force my eyes open wide, blinking quickly. Twice in a row. Again. And again. Please, Brae, look at me. Blink twice. Blink twice.

"Brae," a voice I can't see. "Look."

His face is there again, and I blink twice, and again. He sees it. *He can see me.* He knows. Leaning close, he cups my face with his hands. "Kari," he breathes. "Are you saying yes? If you are, blink three times for me."

One.

Two.

Three.

Brae's lips crash down on mine, and in that place where my body is, he tastes like honey. Magic burns through me again, pain, but this time not all pain. Bright magic and cool magic and pale silver magic I haven't felt before.

Aeric, I can see him now. He leans down and presses his lips to mine, flooding me with power, and I can remember it. The pleasure. I can feel it when his mouth moves across my skin and down to my nipples. A third set of hands touch me, combined with that smooth silver magic. Verys's hands on my shoulders, smoothing his hands over my skin in comforting repetitive motions.

I'm slipping backwards, I think. That's how it

feels, this pull back towards darkness and blankness. The comforting black.

Pleasure slams through me, and I'm propelled back into my body. It's all too much, the world like this. Too loud, too bright, too much magic and pain and the pleasure coating all of it on top but I'm *alive*. I can feel it. I can move my fingers, barely.

Three strands of magic are raging inside me, curling together and morphing into a bonfire that's rebuilding me. Making tethers that are holding me here in the world. I can feel them weaving into place. I'm alive.

I'm alive.

And I can feel everything. Aeric's lips and tongue as he drags them between my breasts and down to my belly button and back. Very's hands on my arms and shoulders, adding touch, stimulation.

And Brae's cock.

Oh fuck.

Magic erupts inside me, sending power shaking through every cell. Light reflects off Brae's face above me as he moves. He's fucking me, cock plunging deep in long, even strokes that fill me up in ways that I didn't think were possible. He asked me, and I said yes. That blast of magic that brought me back was him entering me for the first time.

I shudder, closing my eyes against the brightening magic. God, *yes*. Every stroke shoves more power inside me, connects us, anchors me back in the world. I feel myself coming back. No longer pulled towards that darkness, and I want more. Every step I take away from death brings my arousal back to life, and I feel every inch of him more acutely. Every touch from the three of them, every bit of magic that they offer to me.

I almost want to laugh. Never in my wildest dreams did I think I would be the kind of girl to have a threesome. Hell, a foursome. But here I am. Pleasure settles over me like a cloud and roots itself in me. My back arches off the ground as a lash of fire whips through my soul, the last tether to that dark place breaking and setting me free. I'm fully back in my body and it is thrumming with need.

Brae is long and thick, slamming into me with fierce determination. I know that he's doing this to save my life, but every fantasy I've had of this man —these men—is coming true. I want it so fucking much, even if it's just this one time. I love the way my body is careening through pleasure and not yet falling into it. Savoring it, even if it's just once. I wish I could see the way his cock looks as it's fucking me.

Why do I have my eyes closed when I could see this? They fly open, and he's right there, face so close. He's the only one touching me now, body pressed against mine as he fucks. There's so much emotion on his face, it makes my chest ache. Need and relief and desire. Even anger.

His mouth slants across mine in a bruising kiss. He says everything with it. They will not let me go. They will do whatever it takes to keep me here and safe. Brae lifts my legs around his hips so he can plunge deeper, faster, and harder.

Ecstasy so complete shatters through me, washing magic through every part of me, healing and lifting me up. Pleasure that's a cascade of color and magic my voice comes back at that moment, tearing free of what was holding it back. Yes. Please. More. Don't let it end.

Brae hammers his cock into me, extending my pleasure with every thrust of his hips. He braces himself on his arms above me, groaning, his rhythm faltering as he finds his own climax. Heat and pure, honey, magic surge through me—the magic created by our combined pleasure. He pours it all into me.

The light on his face grows brighter, and I realize that it's me. I'm glowing. Shimmering with the storm of magic inside me. I can't contain it all, so I'm lit up like a firework. Slowly, carefully, I lift my hand to see it. It's strange and beautiful. I can almost see the glittering flow of it beneath my skin the way I can feel it moving. Seeking, healing, restoring.

Softly, Brae kisses me. It's a kiss that makes my chest ache with longing for something that I can't name. He slips away from me, and already I miss his warmth. But he's exhausted. He lays down beside me, breathing heavily, but face still turned towards me. His hand still rests on my stomach, and I realize that he's making sure that I'm still breathing. "Thank you," I whisper.

He says nothing, but nods, just a little, and his eyes close.

Brae's absence above me has revealed Kent, who's staring down at me a few feet away. His expression is pure agony. It was his voice that I heard.

Kari, please. Don't let go. Come back.

Is she gone?

He thought I'd died. That I'd left him. Pain spikes through my chest, but it's not from the curse, it's just me. If I'd fallen over the cliff and left them...

Tears blur my eyes and I reach my hand out to him, as far as I can manage. I'm alive, and I'm not in pain, but that's about it. I have no strength left in my body. But Kent's hand finds mine, and he kisses it. "I'm sorry," he says. "I would help if I could."

"I know," I say. My voice is a dry husk of its

former self. It sounds like dried leaves blowing along the streets of New York in Autumn—just the bare remnant of life. I'll recover. For now, this will have to be enough.

Verys steps behind Kent and puts his hands on his shoulders. Kent goes deathly still like he's been electrocuted. "Help her," he whispers to Kent.

Kent looks at me, sudden awe dawning in his eyes. He doesn't move, and Verys says it again, louder this time. "Help her."

Where his skin is touching mine, I feel the silvery magic of Verys brush against me, and I understand. Verys has given his magic to Kent so that he can pleasure me, be a part of this. "Yes," I say. Of course.

Kent strips his shirt over his head and sheds his pants just as quickly. Of all the times I've imagined seeing him naked, I never thought it would be like this. But it doesn't change how fucking beautiful he is. Perfect olive skin and smooth lines run down his body. It's packed with muscle, built in ways I hadn't pictured. Everything from his arms to that delicious line on his hips is sculpted. And his cock stands straight away from his body, proud and thick as he kneels between my legs.

Shivers run down my skin in anticipation. I like the sight of him above me, taking just a moment to take me in below him before he nudges into me. He's not quite as long, but thicker than Brae is, and I'm stretched by him as he slowly eases himself inside.

Verys has moved with him, standing behind with a hand still on his shoulder, passing the magic that I feel flowing through Kent into me. I lock eyes with him, and I try to tell him thank you with my gaze. I hope that he understands.

I squeeze down on Kent's cock, and he growls, still sinking in as deep as he can go. The thick weight of him inside me is delicious. By the time he's all the way inside me I'm short of breath because of how stuffed I feel. Even without the trickle of shining magic that's swirling between us, this feels entirely different.

Kent's head drops forward, looking at where we're joined together, and then he looks at me. His eyes are shining with emotion, and it sings between us, the magic drawing us closer together. He pulls back just an inch before sinking all the way back in. The slow friction sends quaking waves of pleasure along my limbs, slow, rumbling, and deep.

Slowly, Kent starts to build a rhythm. The magic grows brighter with every movement of his hips, and the way he's filling me has me panting with need. He rolls his hips, changing his angle until I gasp, and moan. My voice sounds a little fuller now, more like myself. Just making that sound changes something, and Kent suddenly plunges harder. With more force. The magic building between us is glowing under my skin again, reflecting off his face and lighting up those dark eyes that I love so much.

Brae draws himself closer to my side, wrapping his arm fully around my waist. I turn my head to his, and he catches my lips in a kiss. The addition of his sunny power has me groaning into his mouth. His hand slides up my skin, across my chest until it reaches my neck. He grips me there, holding me in place while he plunders my mouth with lips and tongue.

More hands on my skin, Aeric smoothing them down to my stomach and lower. Teasing just above my mound, not quite touching. So close to where Kent is fucking that I wouldn't be able to breathe even if Brae weren't stealing all of my air.

Kent's hands land on my hips, pulling me onto his cock even as he slams in. He keeps that angle that sends sparks soaring through me like a bonfire, and I have to cry out. To scream. Yes. The sounds are lost in Brae's mouth until he releases me, moving to my neck to lick my throat. He's tasting my voice, tongue painting me with magic that sinks through me and makes my voice louder, fuller.

I'm so close, hovering on the delicious edge of orgasm. Kent is fucking hard, plunging into me with raw, brutal strength, and I hold on. I don't want it to stop. I could bathe in this feeling of tongue and hands and cock and *magic*. My voice breaks but I can't stop telling them yes. Begging them please for more.

Aeric slides his hand lower, fingers seeking and finding my clit. I'm sensitive and ready, pleasure spiraling deep into my gut. He circles it with his fingers, not relenting, leaning down to place a kiss directly between my breasts.

That pleasure has coiled up so tight I think that I might break. I'm riding the line of it, the dragging sensation of Kent's fucking holding me there. Then Aeric moves his fingers once more, and I'm lost. Pleasure fractures outward, and my voice echoes off of white stone. My vision fires white and dark, consumed by colors as the pleasure takes me. Every sensation is overwhelming. Brae's lips on my skin and Aeric's damned clever fingers.

I'm shaking with it, falling into a new void, but this one feels amazing. I'm floating on it. Silver magic cascades over me as Kent comes, thrusting balls deep and holding himself there, cock jerking with that heat and power. His fingers are gripping my hips so hard he might leave marks. I hope he does—I want to see his hands on my skin.

Aeric doesn't stop teasing me, drawing out aftershocks of pleasure that flicker and spark over my body. Kent has nearly collapsed on top of me, spent from his magically fueled orgasm. Brae drapes his arm across me again, offering the pleasure of warmth and comfort. Aeric stops teasing me, instead stroking his hands over my skin in long motions meant to soothe and relax.

I feel better. Not well by any stretch. I can still feel the weakness of death clinging to me. But I think I might be able to stand. Maybe move.

I can't believe that this is real. We're all together, sitting, breathing, relaxing in the fading glow of magic and sex. Even after they've all shown me in no uncertain terms that they want me, my mind still can't wrap around it. Things like this don't happen to me. I've never been lucky.

Considering that I was nearly just killed, and am being stalked by a homicidal fae female, you could say that I'm still extremely unlucky. But right now, in this moment, cradled by these men, it doesn't feel that way.

Part of it is the heightened circumstances. No one could deny that the five of us have been through hell together at this point. And I love this. I love that they're willing to do this for me. But once we reach the Carnal Court, and I'm healed, it will all be over. I'm a human.

There's a pang of sadness in my chest that I try to push aside. But it lodges there, refusing to be ignored. It doesn't matter if they want me now, they won't. They've claimed a duty to see me healed, and they're going to do it. But after...

I shove the thought out of my head. No. I'm not going to think about that now. I won't do it, because in spite of myself and the danger to my life I don't want this to end. I don't.

Verys, the only one who's still fully dressed and standing, steps close to me. He gathers me up in his arms. Picks me up as if I weigh nothing. "We must go," he says quietly to the others. "Return to the horses, move quickly."

That stirs the rest of the men to action, pulling on clothes and grabbing mine. And then we're moving, speeding back towards camp as if that bitch is on our heels, which she might be, if she heard my screams.

No one says out loud the reason that we need to move and have no more time. If she realizes she hasn't killed me, she'll come back. And I won't survive this another time.

CHAPTER TWENTY-FOUR

KARI

We fly.

At least it feels that way. The fae horses can ride farther and faster than horses in the human world, and we can't afford to stop. Thankfully, the amount of magic that was forced into my body is enough for now. So there is no rest. Not a lot of it, anyway. I made sure that when we returned to our belongings that they helped me find the little box I was given in the Crystal Court. None of them ask what it is—none of them need to.

The herbs are bitter, but I swallow them.

I'm not strong enough to ride on my own anymore, but I don't mind riding with the others. They've kept me wrapped in blankets, extra clothes, and anything they can find. Even with my clothes and the extra layers, I can't seem to get warm. But these men are like furnaces, and resting against them is heaven.

I ride with Verys that first day, when my strength is highest. He didn't let me out of his arms on the way back to our camp or when we restarted our journey. No one protested. He's still the only one I haven't shared any physical touch with, and I want to know why. We haven't had the chance to speak about it, and he wants me—I know he does.

I want him too. He's gorgeous and kind. I still think of him as my angel, from when I woke up in his arms in the jungle. So when he picks me up and settles me across his legs to ride near fade of the second day, I decide to ask him, finally. We're going a little more slowly for this portion, taking the time to rest the horses. They're amazing, but they don't have infinite strength.

"Verys," I say, keeping my voice low.

"Yes?"

I hesitate, not sure exactly how to put the question into words. It comes out differently than I expect. "What do you see when you look at me?"

He looks down at me, caught off guard by my question. "What do you mean?"

"I mean," I say, licking my lips. "I see the way you look at me. You like what you see. You said as much before. But you haven't touched me or offered me pleasure."

"I'm touching you now," he says, intentionally tightening his arm around my waist.

I make a face. "You know that's not what I mean."

"I do know," he says. "And the answer is...complicated."

"I have time."

He sighs, and I wonder if I should be pushing him to tell me something that he's not ready for. "What do you know about fae magic?"

That's not the question I was expecting. "Honestly, not that much."

"I won't bore you with all the small details, but for the most part, magic is dictated by your Court. Handed down from your parents. There are rare cases where Allwyn chooses something very different for you, but that is rare. In the case of fae hybrids, Allwyn chooses which magic you get to keep—which will be the Court your power flows from."

"You're a hybrid?" I ask, guessing since he was careful to mention it.

"I am. But I didn't know. Not until the magic I had thought was mine was ripped away and replaced with Carnal magic."

"Which Court were you?"

He clears his throat. "I was born in the Lunar Court. My mother broke her vows to her husband and conceived me with a man of the Carnal Court. Brae's father."

My eyebrows rise in surprise. "You are brothers?"

"Half, but yes."

I hadn't known. I feel like I should have. Not that we've had a lot of time for me to ask about everyone's family history. It just makes me remember how little we truly know each other and how much more I want to know. "What does this, or the fact that you're Brae's brother, have to do with me?"

"I'm celibate," he says. "I have been since the day I joined the Carnal Court."

My mouth opens and closes again. This conversation is going in a very different direction than I expected. Every one of these fae absolutely embodies sex. Verys included. And if his magic flows from the Carnal Court, being celibate must be awful. "Why?"

"I hope that you get to see the Lunar Court some day," he says softly. "It's beautiful. I loved it there. I had friends, and I loved the magic. But when my magic changed Courts, everything changed. My mother's husband threw me out when he found out that I wasn't his son. For a while I lived with Brae and his family, but everything that I knew, what I thought of as mine, was gone."

"I'm sorry." I ache for him and the sadness in his voice. This isn't a wound that has gone away.

"I didn't want any part of this new Court that took everything from me. So I made the choice to become celibate. It's been a long time now. Old habits die hard."

"So you're saying—"

"That I would break my celibacy for you?" His mouth tips up into a smile. "Yes, Kari."

My body goes hot with a blush. He's seen me naked and helped another male fuck me, and somehow this feels just as intimate. "Have you always been?"

Verys slowly nods his head. "Yes."

"Oh," I say. "Wow."

He laughs again. "I'm used to it now, it's been hundreds of years."

I blink. "Hundreds of years?"

He smiles at me again. "Still young, for a Fae."

Somehow, it didn't occur to me that these men had been alive for centuries. The thought doesn't bother me though. They can't change who they are any more than I can. "I can't imagine going hundreds of years without sex. Or magic."

"I have some magic," he admits. "All Fae do. But you are correct, it is limited."

"Your magic feels nice," I tell him, leaning my head on his shoulder. "Smooth and silvery."

He laughs, the vibration humming under my ear. "Thank you."

I'm not going to rush him. If he needs time to accept that he no longer wants to be celibate, that's fine. That's a deeper reason than I had thought, and not one that you can just turn your back on after centuries. But that doesn't stop my mind from spinning images of what we'll be like together when he finally chooses to break that barrier.

They're good images—his pale skin on mine, silver haze of power carrying us both into ecstasy. He doesn't have to fuck me, but I tilt my face up to his. "Will you kiss me?" Silver eyes find mine, and I see him swallow. "You don't have to," I say. "If you're not ready."

His lips meet mine softly, barely a caress. It's electric, the hairs on my arms standing up in response. I press my mouth up to his more firmly, so we're connected, but no further. We're suspended in the moment before it breaks, and I smile at him. "Thank you."

Verys looks amused. "You're welcome."

We ride again for a while before the thought pops into my head. The story I wanted to ask about. "Can I ask you something else?"

"Of course."

"When we were in the Crystal Court, I saw the story of the Goddess in their windows and their temple. But I don't know the story. It didn't seem like a good time to ask for details."

He smiles and calls forward. "Brae." His half-brother turns back towards us, a question on his face. "Kari wants to hear the story of the Goddess." To me, Verys says, "Brae loves this story."

And it's true, Brae's face lights up. "That's an excellent story, and by the time we're finished the horses will be rested enough."

"You don't tell it well," Aeric says, though I can see he's only saying it to rile Brae up.

Brae narrows his eyes. "I'm an excellent storyteller, thank you very much. This will be interesting for you, Kari, given you're a human who has magic. It's part of your history as well as ours."

"Oh, okay," I say. My own magic was small enough that I hadn't felt it or tried to use it since all this happened. It's the first thing to be stolen by the curse, feeding on my magic, and then theirs. The pain was too much for me to even try to touch it in the beginning and now their magic is so overwhelming that I haven't felt the need to use it.

Because there's enough magic floating in me right now to set a city on fire, mine is safe and protected. I can feel it humming in my chest, a small, soothing part of myself that's always been there.

Brae begins. "This is the way it has been told to me. But you should also know that as with all stories of this kind, there are things that have warped and changed along the way. A long time ago—"

"In a galaxy far, far, away." Kent says. I laugh, but the other men don't. "Seriously," Kent says. "You guys have been around humans long enough to know what Star Wars is."

They shake their heads. "I have a feeling Kent and I are going to have to educate you when it comes to movies."

"We've seen some," Aeric says, tone defensive.

"A long time ago," Brae says louder, making sure we get that he's going to tell the rest of his story now. "There was no barrier between Allwyn and the human realm. It was one world, and gods roamed the land they had created."

A hush falls over the group, and I listen. This isn't like any version I've heard of Allwyn before now.

"Everyone lived together. Humans and Fae, spirits and animals. The gods. Everyone went where they wished. They loved whom they wished, which is how why there are some humans with magic now. The little power you have is ancient, Kari.

"The world was beautiful, but it was not balanced. The gods, holding the most power, ruled. And they were mercurial. Life meant nothing to them when they could create it and destroy it on a whim.

"But there were those among the gods who cared for their creations and felt that every species should be free to determine their own fate. So, after a long time deciding, the gods removed themselves from the world, and secluded themselves in heaven where they could create and destroy to their heart's content.

"Yet the world was still not balanced. The Fae, now holding the most power, ruled. Because humans do not possess magic, they were taken advantage of. They were slaves and servants. They were not allowed to progress in their own culture because they were serving others. But humans were more numerous, and they fought back.

"The fae drew apart from humanity, lived in secret, creating the divide we now have between your realm and ours. This is where many of your fairy tales and legends come from. Some of them are formed with a core of truth. Others are not."

"I don't think I'll ever forgive humans for making us look like tiny butterflies," Aeric says, smiling. But no one else is.

Brae looks at me, his face grim. "I'm afraid that is the best part of the story."

My stomach drops, the seriousness with which he says it. That part wasn't particularly bad, but it wasn't good either.

"The gods' power began to falter without a connection to this world that they had created. For they had used their essence to build this universe, and the separation weakened them. And the division of Allwyn and the human world weakened them further. They started to die," he says, voice low and urgent.

He really is an excellent storyteller.

"For an immortal god, death is unthinkable. But as more of them faded and did not reappear, the gods became more restless. They began to panic. Most of them wanted to raze this universe and reclaim the power they had spent. Start again and create a world that did not steal from them as this one had.

"Only one Goddess—Cerys—and her four husbands, stood against the tide of gods."

I freeze. "Four husbands?" The words fly out of my mouth before I can stop them.

All the men look at me, the faces of the fae males far too innocent. Verys has an amused smile on his face. "That's right."

I glance over at Kent, and he's looking at me. He doesn't look upset, just curious. The Goddess of this world had four lovers. Not just lovers, *husbands*. No wonder that Merina and Kaya were telling me that those kinds of relationships are common and accepted here. I shove down the idea that's forming, focusing on Brae again. He's studying me, waiting until I'm ready to continue the story. "What happened?"

"There was a war. It lasted hundreds of years, with Cerys and her husbands united with the fae against the rest of the gods. Eventually Cerys realized that there would be no winning the war in a fair fight. The gods were powerful, and though she knew they could be held off until they all faded, this world would be destroyed.

"And so she remade Allwyn. Her husbands held off her enemies while she used every part of her power to remake this world and bind herself to it. Her power burned around her, as she sacrificed herself to it. The gods had nothing left to sustain them, and they crumbled into dust. But Cerys herself was gone too, her life poured into her creation."

Brae lets those words hang in the air. That was the image that I had seen in glass and in the temple—the Goddess being consumed by what I now knew were her own flames. I am no longer surprised by Nissa's reaction to the image. The Goddess gave her life so that fae—and by extension, humans—could live. That's a debt that can never be repaid.

"And after?" I ask softly.

"Her body was laid to rest in the Heart of Allwyn, where it is still. Her presence is the power that sustains Allwyn, and the source of all fae magic. They are one and the same."

I nod. It's a lot to take in. "And her husbands?"

"They are the ones that buried her," Aeric says. "Shortly after they surrendered their power to Allwyn so that they could join her. Though it's said that their spirits remain to guard her body."

"That's really sad."

"In some ways, yes," Brae says. "But the Goddess has also protected life that would have been extinguished, created new life, freed the world, and taught us the beauty of sacrifice."

We stop briefly so that I can be passed to Brae and let Verys's horse have a rest from carrying two people. Brae is a completely different kind of warmth, and as we begin to gallop again, I let myself drift.

I slip in and out of rest, my body still healing from what Ariana did. I can still feel that crystal inside me, lurking and burning in moments when the magic isn't enough. That feeling is terrifying. Because I know what comes after it now, and I don't ever want to go back.

That was too close, and it's coming back too soon. I can feel it rising up and trying to consume me.

As we ride, I catch glimpses of other Kingdoms. A city in the distance that lights up the black night sky with thousands of neon lights. Trees and hills that seem to be made of paper, the sounds rustling in the air. Lush and humid air fills my lungs with the scent of water as we pass a still lake that disappears into the infinite distance.

And finally, when the sky is brightening, the sky turns to crimson, and Brae breathes a sigh of relief. "Welcome to the Kingdom of Pleasure," he says quietly.

I look around and take it in as it passes by. I'm not sure what I thought it would be, but it seems shockingly…normal. But everything is *more*. The colors are more vibrant, the scent of the air delicious, even the way the light falls through the trees is beautiful.

There are different kinds of pleasure, and this land is made to cater to all the senses.

Softness and light and flowering trees in colors I could never dream of surround a shining city with walls that look like pearls. Brae tells me that it is the Court of Love, and I wish that we had time to stop and see it. Petals swirl in a rippling hurricane around us while we ride by. Some of them get caught in the blankets I'm wrapped in. Turquoise and lime and deep, blood red.

My stomach lurches with pain, and I have to close my eyes for a moment. The magic they gave me is fading quickly, being pulled into nothing. I'm dizzy and sick, the motion of our riding only making it worse. Focus on something else. Anything else.

The landscape quickly changes to something stark, but equally beautiful. Everything is sharper here, with rich colors and deeper shadows. We pass a Court that is as stunning as it is captivating. Black walls that seem out of place with the environment surrounding it. Spires that look like thorns in filigree, curving and twisting upward, reaching for the sky.

"The Court of Dominance," Brae whispers. His breath sends a shiver down my spine. Or maybe it's the thought of that place. I imagine it would be both sexy and terrifying at once.

Everything changes around us once again and all I can think to describe it is *lush*. Surrounding us are clearings with waterfalls and soft grass. Trees with ample shade and willows that would be amazing to spend an afternoon under.

My body rebels against what it sees. Everything that I'm looking at speaks of comfort and happiness, but my bones have turned back into glass. I'm holding onto Brae, hoping that our pace doesn't break me. "Almost there," he murmurs.

It's coming too fast this time. How can I fight it off when it's pulling me down from the inside? Making me collapse in on myself?

"There," he says, and I force my eyes open.

The walls of the Carnal Court are red. Not the deadly crimson of Ariana's magic, but the supple, deep red of a rose petal. That's all I can see before I'm pulled down again, not pain this time, but emptiness and nausea.

The sound of loud galloping next to us rouses me to look, just for a second, and I see Aeric riding past us at incredible speed, aiming for the Court. I want to take it all in. I want to see this place that we've worked so hard to get to, but the only thing that's keeping me from falling off the horse is focusing on the pressure of my fingers holding on. Biting my lip to keep myself from being sick.

At least we're here.

Squinting my eyes open, I see us pass through the open gates. Pure, delicious, magic washes over me. It's fresh like snow, freeing me of the sickness enough to breathe. And then it fades away, leaving me sicker than I was before. I nearly retch over the side of the horse.

The few things I do see are exquisite. Everything here is elegant and sensual. I catch glimpses of alcoves around fountains. Shining fabric drapes and delightful gardens. Everything is designed to bring you physical pleasure, and it shows. I wish I could focus on it.

The other thing is the sex. In that same alcove with the fountain I see a couple making love slowly. Intentionally. Two females kiss behind the fabric of the drapes, and a mess of fae are tangled together in the garden. So many limbs that I can't discern who's doing what.

Even after everything, it still seems strange to have sex celebrated and embraced so openly. I don't mind. I like it. Could learn to like it, if I survive this. But first I actually have to survive.

The horses stop and Brae gathers me up into his arms as he drops to the ground. Just that movement causes me pain, and I hiss out a breath. I need help. I refuse to think about the alternative.

"Brae." I say his name. It's the only thing I can think of.

"I know."

I can feel myself slipping away as he carries me through the Court.

CHAPTER TWENTY-FIVE

AERIC

I know.

There was a part of me that was waiting, to step inside the walls of the Court and realize that I was mistaken. That the pull I feel towards her was nothing more than circumstance. But it's true.

Kari is my mate.

This gorgeous, precious, fragile human.

Replenishing magic came surging into me the minute I rode through the gates, and that elusive pull suddenly became a thundering current. But she's not just mine. She's all of ours.

You can't walk down a street in any Court in Allwyn without encountering someone who shares a partner. But a shared *mate*? That's impossibly rare. Would she still be my mate if we hadn't gone to

New York? Would we still have a shared one? Would I still have a mate at all?

Some fae never find a mate. It's not something that you can expect, and if it happens, you're lucky. I know that. I'm one of the luckiest bastards there is, even if this is the last thing I wanted. I never wanted to share anyone. I've seen too much sharing in my life, and it's only caused me pain.

But Allwyn—the Goddess—doesn't choose mates for no reason. And even if there weren't a reason, I can't go back now. It doesn't matter what I wanted. This is what I have. I'm in love with Kari. This impossible, magical thing that binds us together isn't going to let me go, and if she dies, the world is going to be ripped out from under me.

It doesn't change how I feel, the frustration of being in a situation that I swore I never would put myself into. But I have to believe that the Goddess, Allwyn, has done this for a reason. Brae and Verys have been my friends for a long time, but now we're more than brothers. I don't have to ask them to know that we're going to do whatever it takes to protect Kari, no matter the cost. Her life is *everything*.

We asked the Rialoir of the Crystal Court to send a message to Urien for us, to inform him what we needed. And I'm riding ahead to make sure that they're ready, and to tell him what happened while we were on the road. He may not be prepared for what this female—Ariana—did to Kari.

I'm glad to be back home. It feels good to have pure magic running under my feet, feel it fully and without strain. I'd barely realized how starved for it I'd become. But being here now feels strange. Everything is different. Changed. I have a mate. The idea of being open in pleasure with anyone who chose me is now unthinkable. I don't know how to operate with this space now, and I haven't even truly been with her yet. Inside her.

Jumping off the horse near the temple, I almost barrel over the priestess at the door. Dark red hair that reminds me of what Kari's looked like before the life was stolen from her, and this female is wearing nothing but the ceremonial marks of her rank. Before, I might have admired her. Thought about an encounter later. But now she doesn't hold a candle to my mate.

She starts to greet me and I cut her off. "I need to speak to Urien."

"He's preparing for a healing and can't be disturbed."

"I'm the one who sent the message. He's going to heal my mate." It's the first time I've said the words out loud, and they ring with special resonance in my head.

The priestess nods, and gestures for me to enter immediately. I remove my clothes, hastily shoving them on an open shelf so I can follow her. I know this temple well, but I don't have time to search the many rooms and alcoves here. The sounds of sex and the rich scent of perfume fill the temple, and I can taste the magic. The air is permeated with it. That's good. Urien is going to need as much as he can get.

She leads me to the center of the temple where there's a large circular space. Right now it's filled with people, everyone connected in some way, pleasuring each other. Visible magic floats above the floor in a haze of color and light. No wonder there's so much magic, Urien has summoned an orgy to prepare.

Across the room, there's an alcove hidden with garnet curtains. It's here that the priestess leads me. I nod to her before slipping through them. This smaller room is circular too, with a simple altar in the center. The room is open to the sky, filling it with the bright.

Urien is kneeling before the altar, head bowed in silent prayer. He's naked. There are no clothes permitted within the temple. "Urien."

He looks up and turns to me. "Aeric," he says. "Is she here?"

"Almost. I rode ahead to make sure that everything was ready."

"I am as prepared as I can be," he says. "Is it as bad as your message indicated?"

I nod. "Yes. And worse. She was attacked on our way here. When we were able to find her again, she was almost gone. We're lucky that she's alive at all."

Urien freezes and looks at me. The look on his face is at once terrified and understanding. "She's reached the gates."

"How do you know?"

"The same way you do," he says. "That was something I did not expect."

Goddess. I close my eyes. Another mate. *What is your plan for us here?* I send the question outward, into the temple where I hope the spirit of the Goddess is listening, along with the prayer that I've been saying every hour since I met Kari. *Please*.

"It's not just us. Brae. Verys too."

He takes in the information better than I would have, simply nodding. We don't have time to ponder it, or hash out what it means for any of us. Because none of this matters right now. None of it will matter at all if we can't save her.

CHAPTER TWENTY-SIX

KARI

The temple is beautiful, from what I can see of it. It looks like a tent, the stone it's carved out of folded to billow like fabric that's every shade of red. Sometimes it morphs through purple into blue and green. But that's all I see as we enter the outer chamber.

There's a soft female voice nearby. "They're waiting for you. Please remove your clothes. And hers."

Rustling fabric sounds around me, and there's a brief moment when I'm lifted into Verys's arms as Brae strips. It's Verys that presses a kiss to my temple, soft and gentle, a wisp of magic flickering into my mind. More heat on my other side. "Kari," Brae says gently, "we need to get you out of your clothes."

I swallow, looking up at him. "I can't stand." I don't even have to try to know that I'll fall if they put me down.

The look on his face is so tender, and so understanding that I shut my eyes again to hide the tears. I hate this. "I know," he says. "I'm going to help you."

His hands are gentle, pulling my shirt up and over my head. I shiver, and Verys holds me closer, wrapping the blanket tighter over my chest. He helps Brae remove my pants and wraps me again. I'm glad that they let me keep the blanket because I'm so cold.

When Verys gives me back to Brae, it feels like being held by a furnace. I like the way his arms feel, even if the only thing I can do to tell him that is press my palm to his heart. He lifts me higher, closer, cradling me so that I can rest my head on his shoulder. "We're here," he whispers. "Just hang on."

We're walking, and I hear moaning. It's getting louder. The distinct sounds of sex and pleasure. And not just one person or one couple or even a small group. This sounds like a crowd. I look just in time to see us walk into a huge space. It reminds me of the temple in the Crystal Court, though there's no statue here. The space is filled with fae in the throes of sexual ecstasy.

Everywhere I look someone is crying out and having an orgasm. The room is bright with magic and heady with sound.

The shock must show on my face, because I feel the vibration of Brae's laugh, even though I can't hear it over the sounds of the orgy. "Are you surprised?" He asks, lips to my ear. "This is the Carnal Court. Sex is just as much a part of worship for us as it is our daily lives. Besides, this is for you."

"For me?" I don't understand.

"They're raising magic. For your healing."

I tuck my head into his neck again, fighting a wave of unexpected emotion. Why would they do that? For a human that they don't know?

Brae carries me across the space, and the others follow. I catch a glimpse of Kent, and he looks as shocked as I do, but he's naked, and he's here with me. That's all that matters. We're careful not to interrupt anything as we move, and I can feel magic thick in the air. But it doesn't affect me. Not yet, anyway.

Verys pushes aside a curtain and we slip into a smaller space. Aeric is standing there with another fae male. He's beautiful. *Beautiful.* He has skin that's the deepest navy blue, like the summer sky, and long hair that's absolutely pure white. I know with bone-deep certainty that this male is going to help me. I'm pulled towards him like I was drawn to the temple in the Crystal Court.

With a sudden burst of clarity, I remember Lai's words there. *Know this: the Goddess is not one of coincidence.*

I didn't understand what he meant then, but now maybe I do. Maybe it wasn't a chance that they saved me. Maybe there's something more to this than mere attraction. Maybe there's magic that I don't understand that put me here and now, in spite of everything that's happened. And this fae male is a part of it. That, I'm certain.

He and Aeric approach me. Aeric takes in my appearance, and I notice that his jaw is clenching, but he doesn't say anything about it. "This is Urien," he says. "The healer we've been telling you about, and our friend."

This close to all of them, including Urien, I'm very aware of the fact that we're all naked together. In a temple that's dripping with sex and magic. I can't even think about what's going to happen, but my body knows. Senses it, growing wet in anticipation.

"Hello, Kari," Urien says. His voice is deep and resonant, filling the room without effort. "May I touch you?"

I nod, and he reaches out, placing one hand on

my forehead, and another on my chest over my heart. There's no doubt that he can feel it pounding, which it is. Because of him. Because of all of them.

His magic enters me, and it's fierce and pure like bright snow and dark like the night wind. It's exactly like the magic I felt when I entered the Court. This time it doesn't make me feel sick. His face fades into a frown. "Yes," he says. "I can feel the curse. And the thing she put inside you. It's siphoning your life force elsewhere." He shows me a small smile. "I do believe that I can sever this curse entirely, but it will take significant magic."

"You mean sex?" I say, by way of clarification.

He smiles wider this time. "Yes. If I have your consent. But it will not just be me. It will be all of us. The combined magic and that of those outside will help us break it."

"Yes," I say. "Please help me."

Urien's hand moves from my heart to my cheek. "I will do everything in my power."

It's not until he moves away that I see the altar in the center of the space. Brae carries me to it, setting me gently down on it. I'm still wrapped in blankets, but they fall away when he sets me down. I can see the scarlet sky above me, bright and deep like blood.

The moment I settle on the altar the thing inside

me twists in rebellion. I hold back the scream that tries to fly from my lips, but I grab Brae's arm and hold it. They all see it, and suddenly they're by my side with frantic looks on their faces.

I'm being scraped from the inside. Emptied faster than I can breathe.

"Urien," Brae says, "It has to be now."

I see his dark face above mine. "I'm sorry our introduction isn't under better circumstances Kari, but I hope to know you better once you're well. Are you ready?"

"Yes." My voice is almost gone. Evaporated.

Urien presses his lips to mine, sweet magic rushing through me, and it begins.

CHAPTER TWENTY-SEVEN

URIEN

The magic writhing under Kari's skin makes me ill. Just being near it makes me want to empty the contents of my stomach, and she's been living with this thing in her body for more than a week.

I study this woman laid out in front of me, and my gut twists. When I received the message from the Crystal Court of an urgent healing, of course I made myself ready. But I didn't expect her to enter the walls of our Court and become my mate. What was just a simple ritual for me is now fueled by desperate, burning need. I know nothing about this woman who's lying on the edge of death. Everything about her is white and pale, from her skin to her eyes, as this curse leeches the life out of her. But I'm going to fight like hell to save her. I'm not going to lose a mate I never had the chance to know. Not when most males don't get the chance to have a mate at all.

The magic I've pushed into her has calmed her, but that thing inside, the physical object, is fighting. Like it knows what's about to happen and that it's about to be utterly extinguished.

I kiss Kari again, harnessing magic from the worshippers outside and letting it funnel through me and into her. It's going to take every effort of mine to do this, and I will need help.

I nod to the others, even the human man who's standing back, watching Kari. He's terrified for her, but I can sense the purity in his desire for her to be healed. I send magic to him too. His need to see her healed alone will bring power to this ritual. When the magic hits him, he briefly looks at me, and nods. He's done this before, then. Likely when they needed to save her life.

Pressing one more kiss to Kari's forehead, I stand back. Being so close to her, I want to touch her. I want to take her in the way she should be taken as a mate—desired, treasured, and truly fucked. My cock is hard, begging to pleasure her. To find my own. But that's not my job at the moment. I stand back as the others approach, gathering magic to me. Harnessing and shaping it.

That's all I can do until I have enough. Until it's ready.

Kari gasps, body going still. A lance of black magic impales her, stabbing outwards from the inside. She screams. *Goddess, no.* I can't afford to be gentle. My hands crash down on her chest and her stomach, allowing the blackness to flow into me.

It's a sea of fire and pain, rotting, burning like acid, breaking my bones. I rip it away from my soul and expel it towards the sky. Even that small taste of it is horrifying. She's experienced this every second. This little human is stronger than any fae I've ever met. And she's mine. Ours.

This little human who is no longer breathing.

Her heart stutters under my fingers. Falters.

Outright terror deadens any pain I feel. I reach out, pulling every fragment of power I can sense into my being, lancing it into Kari's heart. And I form a barrier around that little crystal I can feel inside her. It pulses with a hate so vile I can taste the bitter ash of it. It *beats* against my magic, trying to break free, trying to kill and wither and destroy.

Goddess, I pray. *Help me.*

"Everything," I grit out. "She needs everything."

My words unfreeze the men around me, who went still at the sound of her scream. Their magic joins mine, and she takes a shuddering breath under my hands. Her eyes open, filled with blind tears of pain and despair.

"Kari," I say to her. She doesn't respond.

The human man is the first to touch her, falling to his knees at the end of the altar and burying his face between her thighs. I see Kari gasp, but she's still not present. Yet her body responds to the magic this man wields. I can feel the creation of new magic, spreading and seeping like light across her bones. Good.

Pain spears through my chest, the curse attacking me directly.

This is more than a simple curse. This has sentience. Knowledge. It's figured out that I'm what's holding it back from taking Kari and is trying to bring me down. I squeeze harder with my power, gritting my teeth against the acid dripping through my veins.

Verys touches her with reverence, smoothing his hands down her shoulders to her breasts, around where my hand is sealed over her heart to keep it beating. Verys, who I've never seen touch a woman. Never seen touch anyone. His hands trace lines across her breasts. Perfect, glorious breasts that mold under his hand. Goddess, I can't wait to feel them. He rubs his thumbs across her nipples, and I watch them harden under his hands as he does it again, and again. They rise to perfect peaks, and Kari's lips open, a little gasp of pleasure escaping.

Yes. There.

Verys leans down and flicks his tongue across her breast. I feel the spark of magic he uses with it, joining mine near her heart. He's gentle, teasing her skin softly but earnestly. The tiniest sound comes from Kari, and that sound makes Verys suck harder at her skin, given confidence by her pleasure. His magic catches her pleasure and creates more. I draw it into her heart and keep it there.

Her skin glows under my palm, icy white and pulsing each time her heart beats. That pulse is pure relief. Because every time that glow flickers I know that she's still alive. I can feel it.

Between her legs, the human pulls her deeper against his mouth, adding his fingers to his efforts. He's a natural with the magic he's been given, curling it under inside her and driving her higher towards the first climax. She'll need more than one. It won't be a problem.

Brae joins Verys, covering Kari's other breast with his mouth, and her eyes close this time in pleasure. She's coming back. Her hands reach out, grabbing onto Verys and Brae where she can find their skin. She clings to them like they're an anchor. At this moment, they are.

Aeric is watching her with heat and lust in his eyes, stroking himself. He's gathering his magic, holding back until the last moment. It's a good plan. We share a look, and he nods firmly. This is what we need. Blasts of our power until it all can coalesce. Our fire will burn this out of her.

It will be pure pleasure and pure pain.

Kari's breath goes short, and her heart speeds up, a flash of my own magic breaking through as she comes. It's small, the pleasure bursting up and out in just seconds, but that's all I need. Just that one opening into her pleasure. I thread my magic through it, never taking my eyes off of her face. She's so beautiful, bowled over by the abrupt burst of power. But I stroke it out, extending her orgasm until she's shaking, my power building off of her pleasure and adding to the glow underneath her skin.

When she opens her eyes, she's there. I can see her. "Kari." Her eyes focus on me. "Good."

I lean down close to her face, Brae and Verys pulling back to give me the room I need. "I know it hurts. I know it feels good too, right?"

She nods.

"It's going to hurt," I say, not willing to lie to her. "It's going to hurt more than anything you've ever felt. But it's going to feel so damn good when it's gone."

"Okay." Her voice is nothing but a whisper.

"Do you trust me?"

Eyes closed again. "Yes."

"Thank you." And then I drive magic straight into her chest.

CHAPTER TWENTY-EIGHT

KARI

When I was a child, my family visited France. In one of the cities, I remember there being a wall of flowers in the image of Joan of Arc. She was burning alive. I wondered what it would feel like, in that way that kids do.

Now I know.

The Goddess Cerys burned alive too. Did it feel like this?

The blast of Urien's power shatters through me, electrifying and burning. Purifying. I tip over the edge of orgasm into pleasure and pain, offered up on this altar. I can't change my fate now. It's in their hands.

Kent's mouth is on me, tongue sliding slick and smooth over my clit while I'm wrung out with pleasure. He started it, and Urien finished it, grasping that tendril of sensation and fanning it into a wave. A double-edged sword. As good as this feels, the dark magic is fighting back. I can feel the way it's barely contained, holding me down and trying to strike at my heart.

Urien's magic is the only thing standing between me and death.

Kent stands and Aeric takes his place, plunging into me with one easy stroke. With it comes a pointed crack of power that tumbles through the rest of me, joins and forms under Urien's hands, forcing the darkness back inch by painful inch. But the way Aeric feels is good. So good. Too good.

It echoes that night in the Crystal Court in my mind, the unyielding way he gave me what I needed and took what he wanted. Fingers dig into my hips to hold me still as he fucks me in a ruthless rhythm. Cool, spiced magic billows up from my core, soothing and caressing and sharpening.

Bright rage explodes behind my eyes, dark power fighting back with equal force. I try to hold back the scream, but I just sound strangled. Torture sings along my limbs, battling with that perfect heat building in my core. Pain and pleasure combining so I don't know which is winning.

Kent appears by my side, and his mouth is on mine. He tastes like my sweetness and magic too, plunging into my mouth with his tongue. My moans are lost in him, but he doesn't let go. Instead he pulls me deeper, kissing me until I no longer have the breath to cry out.

Teeth bite down on my nipples, one and then the other. Mouths sucking together. One is a slow and sweetly teasing, the other a frenzied onslaught. Both feel like their lips are on my clit, threading the pleasure out till it's thin as a wire, one tiny breath is all it will take for me to fall off into the sea of heat below.

Aeric is the one who pushes me over. He leans forward, grinding down onto my clit, and the world lights up. Magic and pleasure spiral up my spine, twining outward into the cracks and crevices that I didn't know could feel this good. My body jerks under all of their touch, craving more.

Heat spikes through me when Aeric comes with a shuddering breath. He sinks into me with a final thrust, spilling himself until he's empty. His face has that light on it—I'm glowing again. So much magic. Pulling, twisting, forming a ball of light in the perfect center of me.

Urien's hands leave my skin and for those few seconds he's not touching me it's perfect agony. Darkness explodes, eclipsing all light. And then his hands are on my thighs, magic flowing under his command as he enters me slowly. It's a torturous journey; every inch is being like being impaled with exquisite fire.

I want to pull away. I can't pull away. I want more.

When he's buried inside me, as deep as he can go, he stops. He slides his hands up my ribs so they're once again covering that place where the darkness gathers. I feel so bright, so drowned in magic and pleasure and pain that I'm paralyzed. But Urien isn't. His palm is flat on my stomach. Meeting my gaze, his eyes reflecting the glow of my skin, he nods. "I'm sorry."

He raises his hand, and the world dissolves into nothing but pain. No amount of pleasure or power can fix this. The roar in my ears covers the sound of my screaming. Hands, other hands, come down on mine. Arms wrap and hold me still. There are lips at my ears begging me to hold on and lips on my skin trying to soothe. Nothing helps.

Tendrils of crimson light float up from my skin towards Urien's hand. They coat it like a glove. That thing inside of me grows smaller as he pulls it upwards and out of me. Moving his hips, he forces power into my body. Magic that speaks of winter nights and pillowed whispers. The first crunch of frost and the brightness of new stars.

And still he pulls, the crystal reforming in his palm bit by bit. Every second feels like claws buried in my gut. They pull me apart and shred me to ribbons. I watch that tiny, glowing thing reform in his hand, and I feel my body go still without my consent. I hear my breath stop and my heart skip a beat, and then two.

I feel myself on the edge of falling.

Urien wrenches his hand upward, and it's gone, the crystal in his hand complete and no longer in me. I crash back into my body, residual pain coating my limbs. It's not gone though, the curse. That comes next.

He tosses the crystal aside closes his eyes as he slams in to the hilt. My pleasure is free now, no longer tangled up in that twisted darkness. In what almost feels like rebellion, I come instantly, body quaking.

Magic of every kind is still sliding through me, circling inside, looping up and out and through. I don't stop coming, splashes of pleasure washing over me. I think the world might be made of pleasure now. I can eat it and drink it and breathe it in. Bathe in it and drown in it and still live.

Urien leans over me, pressing a kiss to my stomach while he works towards his own climax. He shudders with it, heat easing through me and showering me with new pleasure. I could stay like this, I think. Caught in an endless loop of orgasms and magic.

All the power in me draws towards my center, packing together, focusing where he kisses my skin. It becomes so dense that it's heavy, weighing me down. I'm glowing so brightly that I'm throwing shadows on the walls. The ball of magic sinks down through me, finding a place I hadn't noticed. That place that's slowly draining me away. Power fills it up and makes it whole again.

I can feel it try to fight back, to take all the magic that's being shoved into it and spirit it away, but there's too much in me now. And with a tiny tremor, that thread snaps.

Leftover magic ricochets around inside me, and I can't see anything but the bright aftermath. The only thought I have as my body sinks into white oblivion is *finally*.

CHAPTER TWENTY-NINE

KARI

I come to consciousness so slowly that my first real thought is wondering if I've been drugged. But no, my mind isn't that cloudy. It just feels like my body hasn't truly rested in weeks, and it finally had the chance—which is true. Even now, I think that if I let myself, I could just fade back down into sleep again.

Instead, I open my eyes.

I'm not in a familiar place. This room is beautiful, from what I can see. Pale, warm walls rise into open archways that look out over a garden that's a tangled, gorgeous mess. The trickling of water can be heard somewhere close.

The kind of light bouncing around the room is bright and clear like morning, and this bed might be the softest thing I've felt in my life.

My next realization is that there's no pain. I don't hurt anywhere. Well, that's not exactly true, since I ache between my legs, undoubtedly from the frantic amount of sex and magic. But there's no magical pain. I don't have the awareness of being drained every second. The relief is so strong that my eyes blur for a second with tears before I blink them away.

I take a deep breath, enjoying the sensation of being able to do that without cringing. There's a weight when I take that breath though. And a very large, male arm attached to that weight, draped across my naked waist, hand spread across my stomach either to feel my breath or to stake a claim. Either could be true with these men. Slowly, still marveling that I can move so freely, I turn over to see which male is in this bed with me.

My body is still weak, but at least this kind of weakness I know I can come back from. I've recovered from injuries before. Sure, I haven't come back from not one but two near-death experiences. But it can't be that different, right?

I complete my turn and find myself face to face with Brae. His eyes are closed, breath even in his sleep. I realize that this is the first time I've seen any of them sleep. They only slept when we stopped, and often I was sleeping then too. He's not wearing a shirt, and I savor the chance to drink him in. Skin that's golden tan and smooth. Muscles that flow from one to the other. They've been so busy giving me pleasure and making sure I'm still alive that I haven't had the chance to explore them. Not that I haven't wanted to.

Reaching out, I press my palm to his chest, feeling the warmth of him and his heartbeat under my hand. Brae jumps, waking at my touch. It takes him a second to realize that I'm staring at him—touching him—and he comes to alertness in an instant, nearly jumping off the bed. "You're awake. Let me get Urien."

"Wait," I say, halting his movement. "Just stay for a second. Please." I want to know about the others, but I also don't want to move. For a few minutes, I want this to be just ours.

He lays back down next to me, not replacing his arm on my waist until I put his hand there. But as soon as he touches my skin, his hand slides up my spine, drawing me close to his body. Oh, I'm so tired I could fall asleep again right now. He's so warm that it's making me drowsy. But I have questions.

"How long?"

"A couple of days. We've taken turns staying with you, to make sure you didn't wake up alone."

I press my forehead into his chest. "I feel like I got hit by a truck."

"I'm not surprised." There's amusement in his voice.

"What happened?"

His hand slides up and down my back, drawing soothing circles. "As far as we know, it's gone. After Urien broke the connection and you'd passed out, we...destroyed that crystal."

The hesitation there tells me there's more to the story, but at least that's gone. "Good."

He laughs softly, but it fades. His lips press against my temple, and his voice is full of emotion. "We were afraid that you wouldn't wake up."

"What? Why?"

"Anything can happen with black magic," he says. "What if the curse was meant to kill you once the connection severed? Or trapped you inside yourself?"

"I'm glad that I didn't know those things were an option," I say, voice muffled because I've tucked my face into his neck. No doubt they didn't tell me because I was already frightened and dying. But it would have been nice to know that it could have been the last time ever seeing them. "Don't hide anything else from me. Please."

"I won't. But there are some things we've agreed to tell you together."

That's fine. I don't care about that. They can talk to me together all they like as long as there aren't any secrets. I've had enough of not knowing things. There are still too many things I don't know about Ariana and why she's doing this for me to accept not knowing.

"Anything else you need to tell me?"

He nods slowly, and I find myself getting lost in warm green eyes. "Magic like that—black magic—always has a cost."

Fear grips me. "Please tell me everyone is all right."

He smiles, like he's happy that's my first thought. "Everyone is fine. But you are different." Grasping my hand, he places it on his chest where I had it when I woke up.

This time I look at my hand, and he's right. It's paler than it should be. I've always been fair, but my skin is *white*. "It started when we brought you back the first time," he says. "When we found you, you were like this. We thought it would go back once we finished the ritual, but it didn't." He pulls a lock of my hair forward, and it's white too. Pale, shimmering softly like tinsel. The memory of color.

"Oh," I say. I should be happy that it wasn't something worse—that the cost wasn't someone's life or senses. But still, there's a pang in my gut. I loved my hair. Being a natural redhead of that shade isn't common. I'd never dyed it. But I'm still grateful. If this has to be the cost, I can live with it. I'll get used to it.

Brae searches my face, seeing if I'm okay. I try to smile, and feel stupid for caring that much. I'll be fine. I will. But the smile doesn't quite make it to my face. He senses it and presses a soft kiss to my lips.

I'm very naked, and he's halfway there, and it's suddenly all I think about. But I'm fixed. There's no reason now, and I can't bear any kisses out of pity. I refuse to assume anything. I pull back, "I'm going to miss that."

"Miss what?"

"I'm not dying," I say. "You don't have a reason to have sex with me anymore. I'll miss it. It was fun." All consuming. Everything I've ever wanted. Something I'm not sure how I'll ever live without.

He laughs softly, but this laugh is deep and sexy. "Kari, why would any of us stop that?" His lips brush mine again, barely a caress. "Did you think that was the only reason?"

"I hoped that it wasn't," I admit.

"It's not. More than you could ever know."

I frown. "What does that mean?"

Brae shakes his head, though his eyes are filled with fire. "This is one of the things we agree to tell you together."

Pressing up against him, I feel how hard he is. I move my hips against his cock, and he stiffens. "Or you could tell me now."

There's a slow smile. "I like you when you're not dying."

"I can show you how much you'll like me," I say.

He rolls over me faster than I can blink, weight pinning me to the bed. I'm too weak to resist him — not that I would want to. His lips drag across my collarbone before he speaks. "Or I can go get Urien so he can make sure you're all right, and you'll find out everything."

I sigh, "Fine."

He chuckles, brushing my ear with his lips. "I'm more than happy to continue this later."

"Promise?"

"I do," he says as he stands off the bed. His words hang in the air, nearly tangible. He disappears, and it's barely two minutes later that I hear footsteps. Urien leads the way into the room, followed quickly by Brae. No one else, yet.

Urien looks up and down my body, and I blush even though the gaze is clinical. I can blush now, without pain. *Thank you*, I say to the Goddess in my mind. And out loud, I say, "Thank you. For what you did."

He kneels beside the bed. "It was my pleasure, Kari." Just like in the temple, he places his hands on my chest and stomach. His magic is so distinct and so clear as it washes through me. Cold winter nights with stars above. Wind and the northern lights. He wields it with precision, searching through me for any signs or remnants of what she did.

I don't feel anything but him. There's no resistance and no agony. Just soothing bliss. "Yes," Urien says. "You are free of it. I wanted to make sure once you woke that there wasn't anything hidden in your consciousness that I missed. You'll still be weak, but there is no magic left in you but your own."

A sigh of relief escapes me, and on its heels comes a wave of emotion. I turn away from both of them and curl my face into the pillows so they don't see the tears spilling down my face.

I'm not a crier. Not normally. But everything I've been holding back—or that was forced down—comes rushing up and out at once. I never wanted to admit how scared I was. The idea of being murdered. I had to hold on and fight as hard as I could. But it's over.

Hands smooth down my back, and I bury my face further, covering it with my hands. I know they know, but I don't want them to see. They've seen me weak enough, they don't need to see this.

The warmth of a body presses against my back, and I feel the mattress dip as the other joins on the bed. Instantly, I'm pressed between them, and I glance up to see Brae in front of me again. I close my eyes, though that doesn't stop the tears from flowing over. "I'm sorry," I say, unable to make my voice louder than a whisper.

"Why would you apologize for this?"

I can't speak. I just shake my head and allow him to cradle me closer. He turns me so that he's pressed against my back. Lifting the hair off my neck, he presses a kiss to my nape, soft and gentle before he pillows my head on his arm. The other one is slung around me just like it was when I woke. The steadiness of his breathing calms me, lets me start to match him.

Urien is in front of me now. His features are beautiful and dark, and I want to taste his lips again. I want to know him in the way that I know the others. He seems to want that too. "Kari," he says, and I'm carried away by that voice. In the human world that voice would win awards and have people begging him to read things to them for the sake of hearing him speak.

One hand cups my face, thumb brushing away a tear. "You were attacked. More than once. There was every chance that you were going to die. Your body was invaded and taken away from you. Those are things that leave a mark. You have nothing to apologize for."

I open my mouth to speak, but he silences me with his lips. Soft and seeking, the tenderness brings a new wave of emotion. Relief and embarrassment and happiness and grief all at once. It's too much.

"Tears are good for you," Urien whispers, simply watching my face. There's no sign of judgment there, or in the kiss that Brae leaves on the side of my neck. I weave my fingers with the ones Brae has spread across my stomach. He holds on as hard as I am.

"But—"

Urien kisses me again, swallowing my protest. If I'm going to be told to stop talking, I can't say that this is a method that I mind that much. He's good at distracting me, making my body want other things.

"I want you to understand something," he says. "I took in that magic to release it. I held it for a few seconds at most, and it was the worst pain that I've felt in my very long life. You bore it for *weeks*. Anyone, fae or human, who would mock you or think you weak for your tears is no one worth your time."

And so I let myself cry. Urien's hands stroke down my side, caressing and soothing while Brae steadies me. I let it all out. The pain and the anger and the grief and the loneliness. Everything that I didn't have time to feel, I pour it out with the tears and let it go.

I'm not sure how long it takes, but when it settles, I feel clear. I'm still weak and utterly exhausted, but my mind is settled. They both can feel the shift in me, and Brae slides our joined hands up and back so he can kiss my palm. Urien offers me a soft, wet cloth to wash my face. I do, ignoring the fact that my eyes must be swollen beyond recognition.

Urien is the first to move, sliding off the bed and offering me his hand. I hate how much I have to lean on him just to stand, but at the same time, it feels *so good* to be upright. "Are there any clothes?"

Brae chuckles. "I don't think anyone would mind if you walked around naked."

I roll my eyes. "You said we have things to talk about. I don't think me being naked is going to help move that conversation forward."

"Fair point," Urien says, gesturing to a darkened archway on the other side of the room.

A soft, warm light appears as I step through it, and my jaw drops. The closet is nearly the size of my apartment back in New York, and it's stuffed with clothes. Not just clothes but *clothes*. Gorgeous dresses along with simpler, more comfortable things. But I'm pretty sure that I couldn't wear all of this in a lifetime. "How?"

"Kaya," Brae says, smirking. "I think she likes you."

I aim for the comfortable things first. Even with these, I could spend forever just marveling at the beautiful fabric and colors. I don't want something that's too strenuous to put on. The two males are pretending like they're not close enough to catch me if I fall, but every time I step they step with me.

I cover the smile as I pull a soft, deep blue shift nightgown and pull it over my head. It falls to my knees and I feel like I'm wearing a cloud. God, if humans knew clothes in Allwyn were this comfortable they'd be storming the gates begging to come in.

Movement catches my gaze out of the corner of my eye, and all the oxygen goes out of me. It's a mirror. It takes up the whole back wall of the closet, and it's me. But not me. I look like a ghost.

I'm skinny like I've never seen myself before, the whiteness of my skin only emphasizing the fact. My hair shimmers prettily, but it's still not *my* hair. I move my hand and the reflection moves with me. But I can't seem to reconcile the woman that's there with who I am. I walk up to the mirror slowly, reaching out to touch it.

My palm lines up with the new reflection. That's me and isn't me. My eyes aren't even the same. No longer green, they're silvery grey now, and swollen from my tears. My lips just barely hold a tinge of pink. The rest of me is white. How can this possibly be me?

Brae steps up behind me, wrapping his arms around my waist. Up against him I look like I was photoshopped into real life. He's too big and too colorful. I'm washed out. Nothing. Even the heat of his embrace doesn't make me feel better. "I look like a skeleton."

"You are stunning," he says. "You're a beautiful woman, Kari. That doesn't change because your hair isn't red. *You* are beautiful."

The words settle in me, and I'm not sure if I believe them completely. But maybe I'll come to see what he sees after I'm used to the stranger in the mirror.

"Do you want to see the house? And everyone else wants to see you too."

"Okay," I say, tearing my eyes away from my image. It feels strange to be doing something normal. To not be running. But I lean on the two of them as they lead me out into the rest of the house.

CHAPTER THIRTY

KARI

This house is amazing. They don't give me a grand tour—I'm sure that will come later, but the small piece that Brae and Urien walk me through is just as lovely as the room I woke up in. There's a courtyard with those same beautiful archways looking out on it, and I see glimpses of more rooms, so very different. In every color and shape, and I know that I'm going to be curious to explore every bit of this place before I leave.

It's easy to walk when I have their strength, down a large set of stairs and into a huge common room, again open to that gigantic garden I saw from the windows upstairs. The first thing I see is what looks like a dining area. A long table filled with an incredible amount of food. Suddenly, I'm ravenous.

I haven't eaten in…days. I was too sick to eat while we were running, and I've been sleeping for at least two. I swear to the Goddess I'm about to stuff my fucking face.

Between us and the dining table there's a large circular section that's stepped down into the floor, filled with couches and pillows in rich colors. It's there that the rest of the guys are waiting for us. They're trying very hard to look casual and failing completely. Aeric is lounging on his side on one to the couches, but the way his body is tense almost makes me laugh. He's clearly posing. Kent is leaning forward, elbows on his knees, rubbing his hands over his face. I can't imagine the state that he's been in, if he thought he was going to lose me again.

Verys looks the most natural, just sitting quietly. But there's tension in him too. When we step into the room, they all look up in unison. "Hi," I say lamely. I can tell that they all want to come over and say hello, but they don't want to overwhelm me. They all stand though, and Brae and Urien help me down the steps into the area with the couches.

Kent steps in front of me, and he reaches out like he wants to touch me. But he hesitates. I nod, and he crushes me to him. So close that I can barely breathe. I don't mind. "I was worried," he whispers. "If you didn't wake up—"

"I know," I say. "But I did."

I sit on the couch near Aeric, who says nothing, but pulls me in for a fierce kiss that says more than words would be able to. And warms me up more than is probably advisable. I should have chosen a thicker nightgown. There's no way that they're not going to notice that my nipples are now standing at attention through this flimsy fabric.

There's a part of me that wants them to notice. I'm nervous about whatever it is that they've agreed to tell me. It could be good—I hope it is—but given my luck recently I'm not exactly holding out hope. But if we're swept away in some sexiness then we won't have to talk about it.

I don't even mean to make to the sound of immediate comfort that comes out of me when I lean back. "This house is amazing," I say. "Where are we?"

Aeric settles behind me as I curl up, letting me lean against him as I bring my feet up. Kent doesn't miss a beat, lifting my feet into his lap, massaging them slowly. *Fuck*. My eyes basically roll back into my head.

"We're still in the Carnal Court," Verys says, appearing in front of me with a plate of food. Including bread and honey. He noticed what I liked at that banquet. This feels crazy. And amazing. In my wildest dreams I never imagined being spoiled like this.

The bread melts on my tongue. It's fucking perfect, and I'm so hungry that I can barely savor it. "This is my home," Urien says.

"Wow," I say.

Aeric laughs softly. "Urien was born a Tiarne—a prince—of the Celestial Court. But his magic chose Carnal. So he's a Tiarne here as well, though he's not part of the line of succession."

I look over at Urien. He has a small smile of embarrassment on his face. "It has its benefits," he says, gesturing to the space around us. "The grounds here are woven with magic. The house and land change to meet the needs of those who live here. It will provide space for everyone to live, and your rooms will be what you desire—even if that desire is not a conscious one. There will always be food. Whatever you need will be provided."

"Okay, I love that," I say. "I need that for my apartment in New York. That will be really helpful." Everyone goes quiet, and it feels like all the air has been sucked out of the room. But I think I'm the only one who doesn't know why. "What's going on?"

Kent's hands have stilled on my feet, and he's

sharing glances with the other men. But he won't look at me. So I look at Urien, "I'm healed, right? It's gone?"

"It is."

"So why is everyone quiet when I talk about going home? She got what she wanted when she tried to kill me, and I'm fixed. Right?" I put down my empty plate on a nearby table.

"It's not that simple," Kent says. "You didn't see what happened."

Urien clears his throat. "The crystal Ariana forced inside you was channeling your vitality away. But it can work both ways. It was clear the way it was fighting back. It would take an extraordinary amount of magic for an object to have that kind of will. And it became clear when we tried to destroy it."

"She manifested," Aeric says. "Just an image of herself, but she saw us, and saw you. And when she left, she pulled as much power as she could manage with her before the crystal was left powerless."

I feel sick to my stomach. So she knows I'm alive. But it doesn't matter. It *shouldn't* matter. She already took everything. "I don't understand. It's over."

"We want you to be able to go home, Kari," Kent

says. "Of course you know I want that. But in the human realm, completely unprotected? There's nothing stopping her from coming back. And you won't—"

He doesn't finish. I won't survive it this time.

Anger floods me in a way it hasn't been able to in a long time. "This is ridiculous. I'm *no one*. Why am I being targeted? Why are any of us? She said there are more, and that human magic was special, but that's it. This isn't fair." I know that I sound like I'm whining, but I don't care. After everything, I should be able to go home. I want to see my shop. I have friends, had a life.

A small voice whispers that if I leave and go home, that means leaving them too. That the life I was living isn't the one I really wanted. But I push that voice down. I haven't gotten that far yet, and this feels like one too many losses.

"We don't know," Brae says. "But we're going to find out. Nothing is going to happen to you. I swear it."

"You can't just keep me here," I say, my voice cracking with the pain and anger that I feel. "That goes against my consent. Your most precious rule. So if I choose to leave, you have to let me. You have to listen to me."

The silence is deadly this time. And Brae's face looks ashen.

Slowly, Aeric slips his hand around my waist. I try to push it away but it's unyielding. "It's true," Aeric says. "We cannot force you to stay. But we hope that you will. None of us wants to see you die."

"Your protection," Urien says, "is not the only reason we want you to stay."

I don't let him continue. "I need to be alone for a few minutes." I stand, and they rise to help me, but I hold up a hand. "I'm fine."

It's not as easy without their help, given the frustrating weakness in my limbs, but I manage. And they let me go. Rage and frustration and sadness are warring inside me as I force myself up the stairs.

Do I really want to leave? No. I can't pretend that I do. After experiencing this, going back to the quiet and frankly lonely life I was living seems nearly impossible. And it might have been wrong of me to just leave like that. But I didn't think I would never be able to go back home.

And maybe that's dramatic of me too. Maybe I'll be able to go back one day. But losing everything when you think it's going to come back to you. Losing everything and realizing that nothing will *ever* be the same takes your breath away. I just need a few minutes by myself to think. Maybe cry again without their eyes on me. Without their kindness and almost unbearable understanding.

I find my way back to my room without much trouble and let myself sink into the piles of pillows and blankets waiting for me.

CHAPTER THIRTY-ONE

KENT

We're all holding our breath as Kari leaves, and none of us speak until it's been long enough that she won't hear.

"That went well," Aeric mutters.

"She's right though," Brae says. "We can't force her to stay here."

"Of course not," Aeric snaps back. "But I'm also not about to let her go off and get herself killed by that bitch."

Verys speaks, voice calm. "No one wants that."

"She doesn't want to leave," I say. The rest of them look at me, expressions ranging from curious to skeptical. "I don't doubt that all of you care for Kari. But you haven't known her as long as I have. She already lost everything once, and she fought to build a life for herself again. It's not that she wants to leave; it's that everything is collapsing around her a second time. There's nothing she can do to stop it because it's not her fault."

Brae nods, and all the other guys look like I've made a fucking lightbulb go off in their head. I can understand why she needed to be alone, but we need to talk to her about this. And she didn't even get a chance to hear the whole fucking mates thing.

I fight down the spike of jealousy in my chest, the way I've been having to since they first told me. When she was still unconscious. I have known her the longest, and the fact that they feel like they have some kind of claim to her irritates me like there's sand in my shoes.

And at the same time, it doesn't. They love her the way I love her. Purely and passionately. And they've shown me that they'll go to the ends of the earth for her. Plus, just like the discussion about going to New York, if Kari told them that she didn't want them, they would back away. Even if it was devastating, they would let her go.

I can't necessarily think it would be the same were this group entirely human.

But if I'm going to be fucking honest with myself, it's not the fact that they love her. It's the fact that I'm human, and I *can't* be her mate. I'm not sure I totally understand all of it, but the way they describe it is almost reverent. A soul-deep connection that—once accepted by both parties—binds you together.

Not every fae is given the gift. Mates are chosen by the Goddess. Or by Allwyn. That's a little fuzzy for me too. But that's the way it is. Sometimes it's clear why people are chosen as mates, and sometimes it's not. But apparently this situation is... rare to say the least.

But the one thing they made sure to tell me was that, as with all things, it has to be chosen. Just because Kari is their mate doesn't mean that she'll want to be. Or is forced to say yes. But still, having that bond with her at all...

I would do almost anything to have that kind of connection with Kari. To know without the shadow of any fucking doubt that we're meant to be in each other's lives. That it was more than just a coincidence that made me go into her shop that day.

"Let me talk to her," I say. "Since she's upset about New York, I'm probably the one that she'll listen to right now."

Urien nods. "Fair enough."

I have the way to her room memorized. I could get there with my eyes closed. We all could, now. There wasn't a second when she was unconscious that she was alone. One of us was always next to her, listening to her breathe. I barely dared to sleep when I was with her, in case I missed something. The relief and thankfulness I felt when Brae came sprinting down the stairs to tell us that she'd woken is not a feeling that I'm going to forget anytime soon.

One of the large double doors to Kari's room is open, and I knock on the frame softly.

"Go away." The response is immediate.

"It's me."

She looks up from where she had her head under a pillow, her now white hair flying madly around her face. I know she's angry and sad, but she's also incredibly cute like that, and I can't help but smile. "Fine," she says. "But just you."

"I'm alone," I say, sitting on the bed near her.

"This is bullshit," she says. Her voice is quiet, almost absent.

I place my hand on her ankle—the only part of her I can reach right now. "You don't have to hide the fact that you're angry from me," I say. "You've earned that much."

"It's *bullshit*," she says, voice much louder now. "Why does stuff keep happening to me? I didn't ask for any of this."

I don't say anything, just watch as she sits up

and forces herself off the bed. She's unsteady on her feet, but I don't intervene. She needs this.

"I didn't ask for that fall. I didn't ask for my entire dance career to be taken away, and it was. Even when I tried, they fucking dropped me anyway. Even though I promised to slow down, to take it slow, they said no.

"So I started over. And you know what, it wasn't perfect. But it was fine. It was getting there. I had you. I still had Emma and Odette. I had customers who liked coming into the shop. It's not like I had any choice in whether or not I was born with magic. *I didn't ask for any of this!*" She collapses on the bed again, and I catch her. Hold her.

I spread her out and roll her underneath me so I can be her shield. I'm not sure if she knows that she needs it, but she does. "It doesn't make sense," she says. "It doesn't. I'm no one."

"You keep saying that. But you've never been no one to me."

"I know." I hate the sadness that's bleeding into her voice. "But in the grand scheme of things I am no one, Kent. Just a former ballerina who happens to be good at making potions. And the only reason I'm good at that is because some human and fairy fucked a thousand years ago, and whoops, there was a baby."

"Stop it," I tell her, putting enough anger in my voice that her eyes snap to mine. "You're saying these things, but I know you don't mean them. You love having magic. I can see it when you work, the joy in your eyes when you tell someone about the ingredients you use and why. And even though it broke you, you're always going to love ballet. I don't know why she picked you, or why we're both here, but we *are*."

I kiss her, taking her lips furiously. Fuck, she's perfect. And I still can't believe that after all this time I'm allowed to kiss her. Touch her. All the things I've wanted for so long. The way her body goes pliant under mine has me hard instantly. I have to wrench my thoughts away from all the things we could do while we're alone. She's still healing and vulnerable, and she needs to be the one that chooses the time and place.

"How can I do this?" She says. "Start over again. Leave everything I've ever known? I don't think I can. It's beautiful here, but how can I just abandon everything?"

"You can do it," I say. "You're not alone. And you're not abandoning anything. Just because you can't go back to New York and live doesn't mean you can't visit. Or that people can't visit you here.

You don't think Emma and Odette would kill to visit Allwyn? And I'll be here too."

Her eyes light up with hope that lodges in my gut. "You will?"

"If you thought that I'd leave you after all this, I don't know what else I can do to convince you."

She's the one who kisses me this time, and she tastes like the honey that she loves so much. The way her tongue keeps up with mine—dancing and twisting and engaging—reminds me how amazing she is. She's not afraid to go after what she wants, and she's absolutely strong enough to rebuild her life. To embrace the changes that have to happen. "Give it a chance," I say. "Listen to what they— what we—have to say."

Kari smiles, amusement now lighting her eyes instead of anger. "You're a part of the 'we' now?"

It seems so fucking strange to acknowledge it, but I am. "Yes."

"Should I be nervous?" She asks, biting her lip, telling me that she already is.

"I don't think you need to be."

She sighs, and pauses. "Okay. Are they going to be mad that I just left like that?"

Pulling her upright, I help her stand. "No one is mad at you for any of this. Especially when you're wearing that." The nightgown would appear chaste on the hanger, but on Kari it's anything but. It reveals the curves that haven't been stolen by the curse and is thin enough that I can feel the gentle heat of her skin when I reach out to touch her.

Kari rolls her eyes and goes to the closet. She pulls the nightgown over her head as she goes, taking any chance of me keeping my dick in check with it. I hear the shuffle of fabric and her muttering about finding something that's going to make us less likely to want to jump her.

I laugh. "What you wear isn't going to make a fucking difference on that front, Kari."

She sticks her tongue out at me when she emerges from the closet more covered, in soft pants and what looks like a very soft brown sweater. "I'm assuming this conversation is going to be about all of us together, and I want to be able to have it without you guys looking at me like you want to eat me."

"I always want to eat you out," I say, thoroughly enjoying the blush on her pale skin. "Come on."

I take her hand and hold it as we head back towards the stairs. I could be completely imagining it, but it looks like she's standing just a little taller.

CHAPTER THIRTY-TWO

KARI

In spite of Kent's reassurance, I have to fight off a wave of embarrassment when we walk back into the common space. But none of the guys even look at me strangely. When I enter the recessed couch area, I intentionally pick a spot that's separate from all of them. I'm not angry anymore, but if I sit near them they're going to touch me, and that's going to be incredibly, deliciously distracting, and I need to focus.

"I'm sorry," I say.

"Please don't be," Verys says. "You have every right to feel what you feel."

I nod. "I know. But you have feelings too and deserve to have them heard. One of you said before I left that my protection isn't the only reason that you want me to stay."

"Yes." It's Urien.

"Why do you want me to stay?"

Kent sits on one of the couches across from me, smiling at me. He's going to wait for them to speak.

"We want you to stay because we want you," Aeric says. Finally, it's out in the open. "We all want you, in every way."

I look around, meeting every man's eyes, and they all nod yes. Bringing my knees up to my chest, I hug them close. "Everything has been pointing to that. I just, I never thought that I would have something like that. How does that work?"

"However we want it to work," Urien says simply. "No shared relationship is the same. We'll have to figure it out as we go, if you're willing."

I'm really blushing now, hiding my face in the space between my knees. "Yes," I say. Even though I'm sad about not being able to go home, I can't imagine leaving. I can't imagine my life without them. Even Urien, though I barely know him. He feels so deeply a part of this, like he's always been here. They're all smiling, so broad that their cheeks must hurt. But Kent is the one who speaks first. "That's not all of it. Tell her the rest."

The rest of them are sharing glances, but no one's talking. It takes a few seconds for me to realize that they're nervous. "Please say something."

Brae clears his throat. "In the Crystal Court, you spoke of what happened before you were attacked. You talked about a burst of magic that you'd never felt before, and that it made you sick."

"Yeah."

"That was us," Aeric says. "It was Brae, Verys, and myself, entering your proximity."

I tilt my head, confused. "The same thing happened when we were riding in. A burst of magic that made me nauseous."

"That was me," Urien says. "You coming close enough to me for the first time."

"We felt a swell of magic as well," Verys says. "When we portaled to New York. We assumed—wrongly—that it was a remnant of that magic."

"Okay," I say. "But why? I've been close to other fae before and I've never felt anything like that."

Brae leans forward, elbows on his knees. "You remember the story of Cerys?"

I nod.

"Her will is woven into the fabric of this land. She exists still, but she and the land are one. She guides the Allwyn and makes the choices we can't. For example, when a hybrid Fae is born, it is Allwyn that chooses which Court the magic aligns with."

I rub my hand across my face. "I feel like we're

going in circles. Please tell me what you're trying to say. I can take it."

Aeric speaks now. "Brae referenced the story of the Goddess because of who she was, and the relationship she had. It's not a common thing, but Allwyn creates bonds between people. Weaves their souls together. Mates them. Some people think that Cerys's husbands were also her mates also, but no one knows that for sure."

Mates. I'd heard of that. It was talked about in human stories of the Fae—Some of the greatest loves of all time were mates. The stories varied on whether it was good or bad. Some of them painted it as the perfect love and everything anyone could wish for. Others a hated thing because it was a bond that was forced.

The puzzle pieces click in my mind. Oh.

Oh.

That can't—can that be true?

Before I even say anything, the rightness of the knowledge lodges itself deep inside me. I thought there was something more between us, but I never imagined that it would be this. I never imagined it *could* be this. "You're saying—"

"We are mates," Brae says.

"All of you? And me?"

"Yes," Urien says.

"That magic you felt was the recognition of it. The start of the connection." Verys says.

"It's also important for you to know," Brae says quickly, "that being someone's mate is not the same as being bonded to them. That must be chosen and sealed by both involved. It can never be forced."

My body heats in a flush. There's a part of me that's immediately aroused by the idea. They would be mine and I would be theirs, closer than any people could ever be in normal circumstances. And another part that's a little freaked out. "But I'm human."

"And?" Aeric asks.

"I didn't know that was possible."

Amusement is obvious on Verys's face. "Neither did we."

Suddenly, Aeric's words from that night make more sense. *This is not the way I would have chosen, but I want you like I've wanted no other woman. And I have finished ignoring fate.*

I swallow, nerves swelling in my gut. I probably shouldn't ask, but I need to anyway. "If you weren't my mates, would you still want me? I'm not going to hold you to something you don't want."

The voices around the room, even Kent's, are nearly in unison. "Yes."

"Okay." I swallow again.

They're all looking at me, waiting for me to say something about how this feels, but I can barely think. This is a lot. Suddenly just to go from the idea of sharing to four of them being mates. A connection that can only get deeper but never go away.

Is that really so bad? The small voice doesn't feel like mine. No, it's not bad, but it's just a lot of change. On top of everything else, it feels too big. Too overwhelming. "I need a second," I say. "I swear I'm fine, I just need air for a minute."

I see them exchange glances once again, but they don't stop me as I walk out into the gardens and quickly lose myself in the myriad of plants. There are roses here of every color I can imagine. The ones I'm most drawn to are a deep purple with a shimmering gold gilding the edges of the petals. There are lilies and honeysuckle and lilacs in colors that would be out of place on earth, plus flowers that I've never seen that must be solely from Allwyn.

Walking down one of the dirt paths, I pass stone benches and trail around trees through the grounds until I'm in a wooded section of the gardens far from the house. I'm thoroughly lost, but I don't care. I need space to think.

The big thing flashing in my mind is *I'm in fucking Allwyn.* How on earth did I get here? How did I go from my store in New York to a mansion in the Carnal Court with five men ready to be with me?

Allwyn weaves souls together when it makes mates. That thought is terrifying and thrilling. I let the idea sink through me slowly. Mated to Aeric, Verys, Brae, and Urien. Every one of them is different, and every one has shown me that they want me in different ways. They've put their life on the line for me.

Even though they weren't forced to.

Because a bond between two people can never be forced, no matter what the magic of Allwyn says.

Happiness bright as the sun rockets through me. *They didn't have to.* They could have walked away at any time, chosen to say no, and they didn't. They want me. All of them. Happy tears blur my vision. Of course I want this. How could I not want this when they're all amazing and perfect and I'm falling in love with all of them?

I know that I'm not ready to be mated. To even comprehend the depth of that, I'm going to need time. But there's no chance in hell that I'm leaving them. I'm staying, and they're going to mine just as much as I am theirs.

I'm going to tell them yes. Yes now, and yes forever.

Magic swirls through me. It's vast and blue, like when you look at an infinite sea. It feels like the deep darkness of a misty forest. The scent of nature and water and danger. The feeling is the thrill of being caught in a wave until it comes crashing down on me, sending me to all fours.

Sickness seizes me, and I heave, gagging on nothing. I'm so dizzy that the world looks like it's spinning. Woah. The magic is gone, but I'm still off-kilter. My balance is entirely gone. It reminds me of when I was a kid and still learning how to turn. How dizzy I would get in ballet class before I learned to spot.

The crunch of leaves makes me look up, and I see him. A fae male, tall and dark, with hair deep blue like the sea. I can feel the hatred rolling off him from here, and the magic that's gathering around me on the ground like a trap ready to spring. This fae didn't come here with any kindness. I force myself off the ground, and I run, cursing the fact that I got so lost.

My body isn't ready for running, and I'm not fast, but I have to try. I just need to make it close enough to the house to call for them. That's all. I can do that.

He's catching up behind me, magic tickling at

my heels. It's taunting me, because he knows that I can't outrun him.

"Don't run."

I push myself faster.

His voice is smooth, hypnotizing. "It will be easier if you just give in, Kari."

My heart skips a beat. He knows my name. How does he know my name?

"I promise not to hurt you. Too badly, anyway."

The magic grabs my feet, tripping me. I collapse to the ground, screaming as I do. There's a flash of wind and movement, and they're there, between me and this male. They stare him down, but Kent is missing. Nowhere.

I'm released of this power, but it's at a cost, because none of the fae are moving. Shakily getting to my feet, I see why. They're bound the way I was. Soft blue magic pulsing around them and holding them in place. All four of them, without a thought.

My heart is pounding, thinking about how powerful this fae must be if he can do this to all of them. Four fae males who are themselves incredibly powerful. "I thought you might try to save her," he says, a cruel smile on his face. "You all are so noble. But Kari is coming with me. And you will not be able to stop it. I would let you say your goodbyes, but I'm afraid I can't trust you to do that."

He's stalking towards me with predatory grace. I don't know what to do. What do I do? If I run, he'll just catch me. But I can't allow myself to be taken this way, because it's her. I *know* it. She sent this male to retrieve me, and if I let him take me, I won't be coming back and this time they won't be able to find me.

I sprint away from him to the side just as he reaches for me, and he growls. The magic chases on my heels again, weaker because he's holding the other's still. *Fuck*. Power pins me to the ground, knocking the breath out of me. It wraps around my wrists and throat, completely immobilizing me and flipping me over so he can see me.

He's beautiful in a harsh way, golden skin and deep blue eyes. Features that could cut something if you tried. That smile ruins everything. It's made of pain and knives and speaks of nothing but vicious, sadistic intent.

Something moves out of the corner of my eye, and I hold my breath. I keep looking at this male. I won't give anything away. It's my only chance. Our only chance. This male looks me up and down with a gaze that makes me wonder if he's imagining me dissected and cut open—nothing more than a body.

Magic disappears as something slams into him from the side, knocking him away and onto the ground. Kent. That blue magic punches straight into his chest and throws him, but then Aeric is there, broken free from the hold and attacking the male with brutal force.

He doesn't have any weapons, but it doesn't seem to matter. Aeric has him on defense. The others are still bound with magic, but I can see it weakening as the move and fight while he's distracted.

Aeric lashes out with a spear of green magic and the intruder barely dodges if, throwing a punch laced with his own power. Aeric simply knocks it to the side. I can't do anything to help the men bound with magic, but Kent isn't moving. I run to him. He's flat on his back but his eyes are open and he's still breathing. "Are you okay?"

"I think so," he grits out. "Hurts like hell."

There's a sound like shattering glass and I turn to see Brae and Verys free of the magic that bound them. Urien is almost there. The intruder has lost. There's a moment when he realizes, leaping back away from Aeric and out of reach of his blows. Brae is already sprinting towards him, magic at the ready.

I see it happen. The decision. When he decides not to take me, but kill me. Thrusting his palm towards me, a spear of raw crackling power roars through the air. It's too fast to stop or move away from it. That will be the end.

But it's not. Verys—moving faster than I've ever seen—calmly steps into the path of the beam. It strikes him in the chest, leveling him to the ground. I don't even have time to scream, but horror fills me as I see him drop like a stone, clothes smoking and body limp.

Urien breaks free of his bonds and the others all look to Verys. In that moment, the intruder disappears. I don't have a single second to spare, throwing myself at Verys with all the speed I can manage. He's unconscious, and his chest is not moving. Not even a flicker of breath or movement.

He's gone.

CHAPTER THIRTY-THREE

KARI

Up until this moment, I never realized how fast fae could move. How slow they had to make themselves to catch up with me. Magic is spewing from Urien's hand and into Verys's chest between the space of me taking a breath. His body barely has the time to heave in a shuddering breath before they're carrying him away from me and I'm scooped up by Aeric, and we're running along with Kent back to the house.

Up and into an unfamiliar room. Verys is already on the bed, Urien standing over him power flowing through his fingers. Verys is breathing. *He's breathing*. That's the first thing I see. Thank the Goddess.

"We don't have time for the temple," Urien says. "He needs magic. Now."

Of course. That means me, and sex. And I would do anything to save him. I'm saying yes to them, and even though part of being mates still gives me pause, they saved me. And I am falling head over heels for each of them.

Verys has been sweet from the second I woke up in his arms. Steady, comforting, and attentive. The thought of losing him is absolutely devastating. It rips through me with fiery pain that will leave a mark if anything happens to him. But Verys hasn't ever done this, and I will assume nothing.

"He needs to tell me," I say. "I need to know that he's okay with this. You know why."

Urien nods, and the magic he's holding brightens to a nova. I can't even look at it as I strip off my clothes, helping Brae get Verys's off. I need him to be alive. I need him to be okay. I need *him*.

He's pouring so much magic into Verys that Urien is panting, but it works. Verys's eyes fly open, wheeling for a second before they lock on me. "We need to heal you. I needed to ask—"

"Yes," he moans, before fading again. His eyes sink closed and the light dims. Yes. I can do this. I climb on top of his body, pressing my lips to his. He doesn't kiss me back, but that doesn't keep me from promising with that kiss that I'll bring him back.

He's mine, and I'm not letting him go. The next time we do this he will be awake to enjoy it.

I reach between us and grasp his cock. Even barely conscious, his body responds to my hand. He's long, growing between my fingers. He's so long that I'm not sure I can take him all. Verys's body reminds me of a swimmer's—long and lean and fit. Perfect. He's pale like me, nearly white from his Lunar heritage. We match.

Using both my hands, I stroke him till he's hard as diamond beneath my fingers and ready for me. It doesn't take long, and I'm reminded what he's offering me, and what I'm taking from him.

I rise up, guiding his cock to my entrance, and slowly, so slowly, take him inside. He feels good, slipping in and making my pussy wetter. I reach out, catching Brae on the shoulder and pulling to me. I kiss him hard on the lips as I sink down further onto Verys. "Magic," I whisper. "Help me save him."

Brae gives it to me, letting his magic pour through me and into his brother. The magic stirs Verys's to life. Yes, this is what we need, for his magic to help save him. Aeric's magic joins Brae's as he puts his hands on my ribs, sliding them around so they're holding my breasts. His teeth bite into my shoulder, and I moan into Brae's mouth. Yes. *Yes*.

I've taken as much of Verys as I can, and he's

still not all the way in. But his cock reaches that place deep inside that I know can light bonfires of pleasure and I'm ready to take us both there. Squeezing down on him, I roll my hips to take him in again, starting slow.

His eyes open, watching me, letting his gaze slip to where Aeric is teasing my nipples, and further to where I'm taking him in. He moans, reaching for me. His hands land on my hips, pulling with what little strength he has.

And so I fuck him harder, riding him in the way I've wanted to for so long. Over and over again, falling down on his cock and taking every inch that I can. His magic mingles with the others, waking up and piercing me, hitting that spot repeatedly until I have to close my eyes. It's too much, and yet I can't stop. I will not stop.

Brae's hand slides down my stomach, reaching me, keeping pace with my riding, and brushes his fingers against my clit. Slow at first, and then faster. And faster still. Pinching down between two fingers, he pulses magic through me, and I come. My spine snaps straight, going utterly still as the ocean of pleasure cascades down like a waterfall. I squeeze Verys's cock with my pussy, hard, the spasms of orgasm wanting more. Magic explodes around me with my pleasure, lighting up my pale skin and plowing through me straight to Verys. He makes another sound of desire, and I can feel just how close he is.

I'm riding him again, lost in the perfect feeling of orgasm after orgasm, his cock hitting me perfectly and the magic looping my pleasure back on itself until it's hard to breathe. Fuck, yes.

Goddess, I throw out the words in my mind as Aeric rolls my nipples through his fingers, adding to that perfect, pleasurable pain. *If you're there, if you've bound us, help me bring him back.*

I slam down on his cock, leaning forward so I can go faster, and Verys goes stiff beneath me, eyes flying wide. He comes.

Torrential, unexplainable power tears through the room. Blinding light like a star turning the world white as Verys cries out his pleasure. His heat gushes into me like a dam has been broken, flooding power and pleasure and pure light through my body. I collapse onto him, unable to move. We're all caught in the glowing storm of it all. I come again, screaming though I can't seem to hear anything, pussy milking what's left of his orgasm from him.

But that's the end. I'm spent. The magic slowly dissipates, and I have spots in my eyes from the brightness. I can't move from where I'm laying on him, cock still buried deep in me. But I don't want to move either. With my head on his chest I can feel the beat of his heart that tells me he's still here.

I turn my head to Urien. "Is he going to be all right?"

His brow is furrowed in concentration. "He's been celibate for hundreds of years. He has not practiced storing magic the way the rest of us have. It's leaving him more quickly than I would like. But he is out of danger, for the moment."

"Thank the Goddess."

"Yes," Urien says, softly. "Thank the Goddess. I have no doubt that she was here."

I had just thought that nova was the unleashing of a magic long buried. That Verys had denied his nature for so long that it eclipsed everything. And maybe that was part of it. But maybe there was something more too. Maybe she answered my prayer in a burst of light.

"I don't want to leave him," I whisper.

I hear Brae's voice behind me. "We didn't leave your side while you slept. You have every right to do the same."

I lower myself to Verys's side, laying my head on his chest and close my eyes, exhausted, worried, and weary. But I can still hear his heart, and that is enough.

"If you call us we will come," Aeric says as they leave the room.

I know they will. They always have. I drift off comforted by the fact that I am not alone, and he is not in danger.

CHAPTER THIRTY-FOUR

KARI

When I wake, the light is dim but brightening. The day is beginning. Verys still sleeps peacefully next to me, breath even and heart steady. Good. He is out of danger. I just have to keep repeating that to myself.

He is out of danger.

I've moved away from him in my sleep, but I move back now, resting my head on his chest once again. I like the steady, even sound of his pulse. It helps me think. My thoughts drift to the others, all four of them. So different, and also so committed to this brand new thing between us. It's fragile and beautiful, and I don't know where it's going. But my stomach flutters when I think about it, and the sense of *rightness* that barrels through me whenever I think about it takes my breath away.

I'm smiling without even realizing it. I have...I don't know what I have. It seems completely inaccurate to call them boyfriends. And I can't call them my mates. Not yet. I'll have to think about that. Somehow I don't think they'd be okay with me calling them the 'man candy crew.'

I lean up, looking at Verys sleeping face. "I'll be back," I tell him, kissing his lips lightly. My stomach is growling, and I want to see if anyone is awake. Yesterday's clothes are still on the floor, and I put them on. Food first, then I'll worry about changing my clothes.

The house is large, and I'm unfamiliar with the layout, but I manage to find my way down to the huge comfy common room, where the scent of human breakfast food is heavy in the air. The dining table is covered with eggs and cheese, bacon and sausage and pancakes, and all the guys are there piling plates full of food.

Kent grins when he spots me. "The whole breakfast table changed, I think because you were craving breakfast."

"I am really hungry," I say, crossing to them. "Verys is still sleeping."

Urien catches me around the waist in a hug. "I checked on him only an hour ago while you were still sleeping too. He's doing well."

My chest eases a bit. I'm glad. Hands pull me out of Urien's grasp, and I'm spun against Aeric's hard body. His mouth crashes down on mine. *Oh.* "Good morning," he says when he pulls away, leaving me breathless and dizzy.

I bite my lip to keep the goofy smile off my face. "Morning."

This really isn't so bad. Most women are lucky enough to find one man to share their life with. I have five.

Brae's kiss is soft, comparatively, as he slides his hand behind my neck and tilts his face to his, but it's deep. It stirs things in me that long for more. My body follows him when he pulls away, and he chuckles. Kent spins me, strawberry already between his lips when he kisses me, sharing the sweetness. I bite down and pull my half away. "Thank you."

"You're welcome." He's grinning, eyes shining and bright and I can't remember the last time I saw him this happy. It makes him look younger.

"I feel left out," Urien says, pulling me once again into his arms. "Good morning." He kisses my forehead first, my eyes flickering closed. Brushes of lips, barely there on my eyelids before his mouth touches mine. Soft and sweet, I welcome that rush of clear, night magic. It's like being kissed by the wind.

"You know how to wake a girl up," I say to no one in particular.

Aeric laughs. "We have other ways to wake you up, too. Believe me."

I blush while I fill my plate with eggs and toast with jam and butter and sausage that smells so good my mouth is watering by the time I sit down.

We're mostly silent while we eat, because the food is so fucking good we can't get a word in. But when our plates are nearly empty, I know that we have to talk. "I was coming back last night," I say, "to keep talking, when everything happened."

Everyone comes alert, acknowledging that we still have important things to discuss. "I'm staying," I say, the blush suddenly fierce on my face. "I...like you all." It's so much more than that, but I can't say that word yet. It's too big and my heart is too full for it. "I'm not ready to be mated, but I want all of you. I want to figure this out together."

Kent is smiling, and Urien reaches out to take my hand before he kisses it. Aeric's look of pure satisfaction and pride tells me enough. Brae looks at me with so much emotion that I have to look away. It makes my heart stutter.

"I have a couple of conditions though."

Aeric speaks. "Name them."

"I need to go back to New York. Not permanently, and not alone. But I need to make arrangements for the shop, and I need to make sure my friends know that I'm okay. They were expecting to see me the night I disappeared."

"That's reasonable," Brae says. "We'll make sure that you can do those things."

"We warded the house while you were sleeping," Urien says. "There won't be any more intruders here. That you can be sure of."

"Good." I'm smiling now, resting on the couch and looking at all of them. It's the first time in forever that I feel *good*. Happy and easy and rested. I almost laugh. All it took was five men to meet those needs.

They look happy too.

"I'm going to go take a bath," I say. "Or a shower. Whatever the magic gave me in my bathroom." The men laugh and Aeric brushes my hip with his fingers as I pass. The simple gesture of affection hits me in my gut and sets my heart pounding.

Five. I have five men.

I head up the stairs and up to the room I've been using. I guess it's mine now.

My body stops on the stairs before I can fully

process the thought. Before I was attacked last night, there was magic. It left me sick and retching on the ground before I saw the intruder. Just like when the others got close enough to me for it to matter.

Goddess, no.

Yes. A small voice whispers back.

My heart is pounding in my ears. My stomach turning with the realization.

I have another mate.

And he tried to kill me.

To Be Continued...

Want to know what happens next? Aeric, Brae, Kent, Verys, and Urien are waiting for you in *Euphoria.*

AUTHOR'S NOTE

Hello my beautiful readers! I hope you enjoyed FEVERED, the first installment in the the Carnal Court Series! This series is really close to my heart, and I love the characters. You'll be seeing more of them very soon!

But I do have one request—if you like this book, would you consider leaving me a review? I love hearing from readers about what they loved, and even what they didn't. Reviews like yours help others find books!

There are more words coming to you very soon, and I hope to see you there.

Devyn Sinclair

KEEP IN TOUCH!

If you want to keep up with me and learn about new releases and hang out with an amazing community of readers, come join my Facebook Reader's Group: Devyn Sinclair's Delightful Deviants. I look forward to meeting you there!

If you'd only like new release announcements or other information, you can sign up for my newsletter through my website—devynsinclair.com—or find me on most social media platforms.

ABOUT THE AUTHOR

Devyn Sinclair writes steamy Reverse Harem romances for your wildest fantasies. Every sexy story is packed with the right amount steam, hot men, and delicious happy endings.

She lives in the wilds of Montana in a small red house with a crazy orange cat. When Devyn's not writing, she spends time outside in big sky country, continues her quest to find the best lemon pastry there is, and buys too many books. (Of course!)

ALSO BY DEVYN SINCLAIR

The Carnal Court

Fevered

Euphoria

Shameless

Breathless

War of Heavenly Fire

Queen of Darkness

Queen of Torment

Queen of Annihilation

The Royal Celestials

The Virgin Queen

Printed in Great Britain
by Amazon